Zeba

AN ACCIDENTAL SUPERHERO

HUMA S QURESHI

HarperCollins *Publishers* India

First published in India by HarperCollins *Publishers* 2024
4th Floor, Tower A, Building No. 10, DLF Cyber City,
DLF Phase II, Gurugram, Haryana – 122002
www.harpercollins.co.in

2 4 6 8 10 9 7 5 3 1

P-ISBN: 978-93-5699-607-6
E-ISBN: 978-93-5699-608-3

Typeset in 11.5/15.2 Scala at
Manipal Technologies Limited, Manipal

Printed and bound at
Thomson Press (India) Ltd.

This book is produced from independently certified FSC® paper
to ensure responsible forest management.

For
all the little girls who dream of flying
and
misfits who refuse to grow up,
I have simply one advice ...
Keep asking those damn questions!

1

9 August 2019

Good evening!

But I should not be starting off with that rather inaccurate and imprecise greeting since it is about 15 minutes past midnight as I write this.

Now, I am in a bit of a predicament. What is the correct way to wish someone a 'good midnight'? Perhaps something along the lines of 'Waddup, Owl?' would be the correct salutation for unholy midnighters... Or 'All midnight-oil burners unite!' Or 'Hey, snooze off!' Or shall I simply and unimaginatively stick to a flavourless 'Hi!'?

When in doubt take the shorter, simpler route, I suppose?

So here goes...

10 August 2019
00:18

Hi!

I'm a second-generation immigrant based in New York, and I love my life. Over the course of this book, I shall share with you how I am also (surprisingly) destined to protect it.

Although I did not start this book with the usual 'Once upon a time blah blah blah' banality, if ever there was a tale that needed this particular opening line, then perhaps it is this one.

You see, I am, after all ... ahem ... a Superhero.

And this story shall take you to the very beginning ... to the source of my superpowers, the fabled holy spring Zsa Zsa, where I shall, eventually, also confront my destiny.

So, yes... I am Zeba, an accidental superhero with a hijab for a cape. Yes, you read that right.

Everything you will read in the following pages is fiction.
Do not believe anything you read here.
Just because something is written doesn't make it true.
Right?

2

An Introduction to a World-Class Superhero

Present Day, 2019

Zeba

Some stories begin as nightmares—dark and deep. They emerge from your subconscious, clawing at your heart, tugging at you from your navel with swift, sharp pulls. You wake up drenched in sweat, heart racing, and you look around, unblinking, trying to grapple with reality. *Was your dreamworld true or is this one?*

Maya. Illusion.

Hard to tell. Hard to comprehend.

But all nightmares bring forth some deep, dark fear. Of losing someone you love, of death, of ageing, of losing all your teeth, of faking an orgasm with cute-but-unimpressive-in-bed Mike, of sitting at the back of a moving car as you watch old loves tearfully wave you goodbye. Forever.

Often, I have a hard time telling apart what is real and what is imaginary. Even when I'm awake. It could be the excessive smoking of weed. I'm not sure. In any case, this weed is lit.

I lie on my rooftop. Sunbathing. Wide hat plopped over my eyes. I swing my feet down from the sunchair and walk barefoot on the fake grass stuck to the floor with some kind of super-strong adhesive. The vertical garden of this lavish thirty-third floor is springing all sorts of lush greenery. I look over the skyline. What an awesome fucking view.

But everywhere, people are just busy being busy. The rusty-red bridge with the snarling New York Traffic crowding it. People running to airports, jobs, families. Mundane. Boring.

Looking down, I take another long drag. So many people below, milling about. A final puff and I flick my joint over the edge and down, and follow its descent. Will it fall on someone's blonde hair extensions or set someone's dress on fire?

NEED. FOR. DRAMA.

It falls on the pavement and I imagine a conscientious brown shoe serendipitously stubbing it out. Damn. What an anti-climax. New York annoys me so much at times. Party poopers. Devoid of drama.

Most of the time, people don't even look at you. One time, after a trip to my dermatologist—who charged me 1,200 dollars for a 'diamond meets platinum meets liquid gold' treatment and smeared a brown shitty-looking cream on my face to numb the sting of the laser—I decided to ditch my car and walk down Lexington Avenue to my favourite protein smoothie place, Equamix.

Navigation is not my strong suit. With Doobie, my devoted black Labrador, on a leash, I buzzed through people. My face covered in what looked like peanut butter. The chunky kind. Not smooth. Nut Butter Co. variety. You get the picture. The dark goo bothered nobody. Heck, no one even gave me a second look. No narrowed eyes in the crowd. No one reacted. Nothing to show that anyone noticed a thing. I could have fallen down, drunk, face first, in an Indian-style latrine and come up with my face covered in potty—potty that looked like it came from someone who ate too much protein and not enough greens. You know what I mean: shit that's darker, almost black, not the soft, yellow type. But nobody cared. Nope. Nada.

Anyway, doing weird shit and pausing to see how people react—that's my favourite pastime.

The chauffeur was waiting with the car outside Equamix. I walked in and ordered the Choco-Nib Almond Milk Vegan Whey Protein Shake, 550 calories, and picked up a box of the overpriced energy bars. I saw hordes of people inside punishing themselves on treadmills, in sessions of hot yoga, Pilates, barre class, kickboxing, boot camp with Cindy, functional with Danny, weight training. I saw them labouring so hard to become fitter, hotter, striving to be better versions of themselves. Fuck, I hate it when people say that and go all Oprah-stic on each other. Fuck that shit.

Repulsed by that 'happy hormone environment', I returned my energy bars and asked for Cheetos instead. The leopard-print-wearing, bikini-bodied struggling model and part-time Equamix server/protein-shake-mixer operator lady looked at me and said with a wink, 'I would NOT eat those, honey.'

Bitch. Judging me. My lack of self-control. My greed for all that dunked-in-artificial-colouring, artificial-preservative-filled junk that Equamix probably did not even stock. What's worse, she masked her judgement under a sweet, saccharine smile.

Bitch. Bitch. Bitch.

I smiled back at her. 'You're right. Self-control can be *so hard*.'

Smiled again.

Bitch. Again.

I left with my 20-dollar protein shake, organic paper straw dangling from my lips. As soon as I exited the building, I threw the shake into a trash can and got into my car.

'Let's go home, Abdul,' I said to my chauffeur.

Being rich and polite is such a pain in the ass.

3

Summer, 1992

The Young Eunuch

Kherun dashed along the palace corridor to fetch the midwife. It was way past midnight, and the labour pains had started suddenly and prematurely. This was sad business. Unexpected, urgent and sad.

The midwife hurried across the palace garden, muttering an old Arabic prayer. Something about new beginnings and souls, about birth and glory. As Kherun ushered her into the bedroom of the wailing, expectant mother, an old wise owl hooted. (Which old owl is not wise?)

'Kherun! Get some hot water and sheets. Lots of sheets!' ordered the midwife.

As Kherun rushed off again, Miriam's scream echoed in the birthing chamber. *Poor girl,* thought Kherun. *It is going to be a long night for her.*

Once the preparations for childbirth were complete, Kherun had little left to do. She held Miriam's hand and occasionally touched her forehead, muttering weak words of reassurance from time to time. In her mind all she could think was, *You poor, poor khanabadosh girl.*

Miriam, a goatherd's daughter, was barely fourteen and in childbirth. Kherun imagined the physical agony the girl was going through would be worse than anything she had ever felt before. *Worse than being taken away from your family at ten years of age. Worse than being forcefully married off to a man three times your age. Worse, perhaps, than the first time he must have forced himself on you.* Kherun shuddered. The thought of the sullen Khan forcing himself on this delicate child made her blood run cold. The Khan had a handsome face, but it was marked by the darkness he held within. Deep lines along the sides of his mouth, a cold gaze and his trademark Pathan nose gave him a formidable appearance.

Maybe, thought Kherun, *the Big Khan did love Miriam. Who knows with these things?*

Although, that seemed unlikely given his sordid reputation. The Khan, their Great Leader and King, had many wives and concubines. But not one of them ever entertained the idea of being loved by him—or even that he was capable of it. Kherun's thoughts wandered. *What must it be like to have a woman's body? To feel a man inside you? Have beautiful, soft breasts? Feel the rigours of childbirth?*

The only times Kherun fought with her Allah were in the dark moments of agony when she was acutely aware that her body would never change. She would never have the curves and crevices that women did. Her voice would never be as sweet as a woman's. She would never know what it is like to bear a child, to give birth, to bring forth the miracle of life. In that moment, Kherun felt a simmering resentment towards the poor, withering girl whose hand she held. At least she didn't have to fight her own body, her own sexuality.

When a baby is born, they are assigned a biological sex – male or female – based on their genitals. But since Kherun was born intersex, with ambiguous private parts, she was branded a hijra at birth. Such children are often referred to as the 'Third Gender' in the Indian subcontinent. Yet, despite her intersex anatomy, Kherun felt every bit a woman and used the pronouns She/Her in Urdu and her native Shina to refer to herself long before it was suitably woke to do so.

A scream.

Miriam's agonized cry jolted Kherun back to the present. She exchanged a knowing look with the midwife. They had suspected this all along: the girl was perhaps too young to survive the night.

A few hours later, a tired and sleep-deprived Kherun rolled a cigarette and lit it. She took a drag and looked up at the night sky. This tobacco was exquisite. Stolen—no, borrowed!—from the King's chamber. The Great Khan smoked the best stuff. He indulged in the best of everything, really. He was the King after all. Those who were loyal to him were rewarded, and his challengers routinely punished—flogged or killed. He was not an easy man or a kind one, but he did have a keen eye that saw through all sorts of bullshit. In the Kingdom of Khudir, there was no hiding from the Great Khan.

Of course, Khudir was a tough kingdom to rule.

Nestled in the rugged Himalayas, surrounded by subcontinent heavyweights India, Pakistan, Afghanistan, and proximate to China and Russia, the kingdom had a turbulent and violent past. There was no doubt it needed a forceful iron hand to govern it, especially since the late 1980s, when the sudden discovery of oil changed everything here. Kherun was no expert in geopolitics, but she understood the tremendous changes that the presence of oil brought to the region and the tsunami of greed and power politics that accompanied it.

Almost overnight, from being a forgotten and impoverished kingdom of nomads and goatherds in the Himalayas, Khudir became a coveted hotspot, rich with oil money, and its new king a powerful, sought-after ally. The West and the kingdom's neighbours wooed him, and he let them. He knew he had a winning hand, and he played his cards right.

The Khan was an ally of the West, and friendly to his neighbours. Often spotted at football games in Europe, at the Grand Prix, and various philanthropic events, he projected an image of being young, progressive and modern.

But the reality was quite different.

At home, his people despised and feared him. Public floggings and hangings were the norm. Yet, the outside world remained oblivious—or perhaps they simply did not care. Taking inspiration from his Taliban allies, he passed laws that stripped the women in his kingdom of basic rights. They were forbidden from going out unaccompanied by a male escort. They were not even allowed to read: any woman found reading a book could lose an eye or a finger.

China
RESTRICTED AREA
KHABA KHATOON HILLS
HAWAL OIL FIELDS
JURELL
BARASHULL
THE CITY OF KHUDIR
SHAH FOREST
ZSA ZSA
CAINTOL
Pakistan
ANANPLAG
ZAGREP
India
The Kingdom of Khudir

Cool king abroad. Despot at home. For the world, the poster boy of the good life. Starving people at home.

Modern Muslim leader overseas. Autocrat at home.

To this chaotic world, to this man, you are born, little child, thought Kherun. *And you are not even aware of it.*

A girl. *Hai, afsos.*

Pity. Pity.

He is not an eager father waiting to know if you are safe and healthy, or how your mother is doing. He is not pacing up and down with anticipation, trepidation, or even the slightest nervous energy. Tonight, as you enter this world, he is not even in the country. Your father is not aware that you were coming—or that you have arrived.

Welcome to the big, bad world, poor baby girl. Welcome to a shit life, thought Kherun. Maybe the child would mercifully die early of polio or chicken pox or cholera or measles or ... whatever else killed infant babies nowadays in mountain kingdoms. Maybe she would survive a miserable childhood only to die just like her teenage mother was going to tonight.

'Treshh!'

Miriam was asking for water. Her lips were cracked. As the midwife handed her some water, the young mother's pretty face drained of colour. Her body went limp, as if unable to carry its petite load anymore. Weakly, she asked for her baby and made a herculean attempt to nurse her. The baby seemed grateful for her first meal. It didn't whimper or cry.

Miriam lay back slowly. Aware that her body was crumbling from inside, having lost a lot of blood. In a soft voice, she mumbled, 'This is not what I wanted. I never got what I wanted. Never. Not even once.'

The midwife tried to pacify her, but the girl went on, delirious, 'Abba. I forgot to shut the sheep pen. Sorry, Abba! Ammi! See my baby, Ammi!'

Suddenly, she stopped and looked wide-eyed at the midwife. 'I'm dying ... Ammi. But I cannot leave my baby behind. Promise me ... promise me that you will kill her before that Shaitan sets his eyes on her. Promise me!'

Both Kherun and the midwife gasped. This was a dreadful wish. Her eyes brimming with tears, the midwife gave Kherun a pleading look and stood aside: she could not be entangled in this mess. Kherun stood next to Miriam in a daze.

'Come closer,' Miriam called out. Kherun knelt by her bedside. 'You saw everything. You know everything. You could not save me, my dear Kheroo Appi. But save her. Please save her.'

Appi. Appa. Elder Sister.

'Tell him it's stillborn. Please. Take her to a well and drown her. Offer her to the Almighty. But don't let him see her.'

With these words, Miriam breathed her last.

CLIP-CLOP. CLIP-CLOP. CLIP-CLOP.

Across the rugged terrain, Kherun rode for her life, her black steed galloping urgently. Sunrise was only a couple of hours away. She needed to reach her destination before that, before anyone spotted her. Under the dark, stormy sky she rode, right up to the mouth of the holy spring Zsa Zsa.

It was in those holy waters that she would lay the baby to rest. It was murder. Infanticide. Kherun knew it was wrong. But it was also a mother's dying wish. Her mind was a whirlpool—of guilt and horror and her commitment to duty.

Meanwhile, back at the palace, the kind midwife was taking care of Miriam's last rites. Washing the body and scenting her. Preparing her before she was laid to rest in a grave. Kherun had had to convince the midwife to tell the palace officials that the baby was stillborn. That both mother and babe had died during childbirth. She knew no one would care.

At first, as Kherun swaddled the baby in layers of cloth, the tender-hearted midwife had protested. *Why not let the baby live? Give her to someone? Hide her!*

But Kherun knew it would be too dangerous. Royal blood given to commoners? It was unthinkable.

If found out, they would both be beheaded for treason, or skinned alive. The Khan might not care about this baby, but the hurt to his honour would be enough for him to hunt down and slaughter all those involved. It was just too risky.

The sky was just about lightening as Kherun reached the holy spring Zsa Zsa. It was dead quiet. She had had to take a longer detour to avoid the guards who protected the entrance to the holy site. Kherun dismounted from the horse and walked towards the spring. This was easily the most difficult thing she had ever had to do in her life. She looked at the horizon and said a soft prayer. For compassion, for forgiveness.

Tearfully, she kissed the baby on the forehead. The baby's face as she slept blissfully, unaware of her fate, tugged at Kherun's heart, but she knew she had to do it. There was no turning back now. Slowly, painfully, reluctantly, she placed the baby in the spring and let her drown.

Kherun fell to the ground, crying. What had she done? How would she ever forgive herself for taking an innocent life? She turned to her Allah, unsure if she could have done anything differently.

Just then, the air resounded with the morning call to prayer. The Azaan.

The sound brought Kherun back to the present. Still unable to stop her tears, she quickly climbed onto her horse and stealthily hurried back to the city. She would have to return before anyone suspected something was amiss. She could not help the feelings of guilt that surged inside her. The baby had come and gone. An escape from this cruel world. An early and quiet departure from all the tyranny and sorrow and fear. Without any fanfare. Without leaving a mark that she had even existed. Without even a name.

A girl without a name died today.

4

Miracle #1

Meanwhile ...

As the baby floated away, the holy waters of Zsa Zsa enveloped her, entering her nostrils, her wailing mouth. Small bubbles rose to the surface as the final reserves of air escaped from her tiny lungs. With a little shudder, the little, lifeless body sank to the bottom of the spring. Motionless, it lay there—a vision of death, angelic beauty and calm. Abandoned, dead, alone.

The Azaan still rang in the air. A call to prayer. God's Word. As the last words of the Azaan came to a haunting end—*Allahhhhhhhhhh Hu Akbar*—something happened. Something inexplicable. Something beautiful.

The gentle winds on the surface blew stronger in swirls. The sky turned dark. A sudden streak of lightning illuminated the surroundings. But this was no ordinary thunderstorm. A second bolt of lightning cut straight through the sky and plunged into the spring, towards the baby. Anyone able to follow its trajectory would see it pierce the baby's heart.

As if a light bulb had been suddenly switched on inside a dark room, the baby opened her eyes wide. **The Divine Spark had put life back into her body**.

She took a deep breath, then using her tiny arms she freed herself from the cloth she was wrapped in. As if they did this every day, her infant legs stretched and paddled as she rose to the surface with amazing ease, emerging above the water with a grateful inhale, gurgling and happy.

Alive.

5

Miracle #2

While the baby gently bobbed on the gurgling waters towards the shore, in the far distance a large boisterous group had gathered. A family had come on a pilgrimage to the holy site at the mouth of Zsa Zsa.

You see, the site that was meant to be the baby's Final Resting Place was in fact a popular place of pilgrimage where locals came to seek blessings. Poor Kherun, in a dilemma and moved by her faith, had chosen this particular spot subconsciously, thinking perhaps that her choice of a blessed location might mitigate her crime in the eyes of God. The fervently religious can believe anything, right? Even that a terrible crime like drowning a baby can be offset somehow or its consequences increasingly diminished if it is committed on a holy site.

Of course, this was also one of the only bodies of water close to the Royal Palace. The other springs and wells en route were likely to have long dried up, with the Great Khan unconcerned about his people having access to clean drinking water.

But, before I proceed further with our story, a short note on Zsa Zsa.

Zsa Zsa is a snow-fed spring that for ages, since the time of the Prophet, Peace Be Upon Him (PBUH), has been revered as special to Muslims across the world. Even now, many people arrive in Khudir from across the world to pay their respects to and drink from this divine source. Khudir is a mountainous, landlocked kingdom, mostly dry and arid; Zsa Zsa is its main source of water. Muslims the world over believe that Zsa Zsa's waters contain the elixir of life, that its holy water can cure ailments and perform miracles. It is from this lonely spot, they claimed, that all life was born. Usual divine water stuff, you know.

Looking at this seemingly ordinary spring it would be hard for naysayers to accept that this is the source of ALL life. But then that has long been the debate between believers and non-believers. Between religion and science.

But faith is faith.

Often, it is our individual human ways of seeing and perceiving that define truth for each of us. Our very personal and relative truth. Our absolute reality. Our Gods. Our God. Our Prophets. Our Prophet. Our heroes. Our saviours. Our. I.

With people eager to test this theory of divinity, Zsa Zsa was often in the academic spotlight. Many scientists took water, mud and rock samples to scientifically determine if the spring truly had any special quality or ability. But they found nothing. Nothing special at all. It was just water. H_2O. Two atoms of hydrogen and one of oxygen. The specimen had a very high pH balance, sure. But it was just water. No human-made instruments could define or calculate the true measure of its divinity or speciality or spirituality or healing powers. The scientists thus concluded that this water was NOT special. And the devotees believed it WAS. And, as the saying goes, the twain would never meet.

I often wonder: How does one measure the divine? How does one prove scientifically that something is unique, out of the ordinary? Which X-ray, MRI scan, blood test, chemical test can 'show' us the divine? Forget divinity, can we even measure what it means to be human? How do we clinically measure kindness? Or anger? If you break open a human skull, can you see a man's dreams? Or his desires? Can you see his guilt? His love? And, if humans cannot define or measure these 'things', can we really refute their existence?

Perhaps we can all agree that there is no reason, no need, to argue at all. Maybe, over the centuries, spiritualists and scientists have all been struggling to describe, study and define the same phenomenon. They just use different terminology, different names and words, to describe the same thing. Maybe the *Godly* and the *Ordinary* are the same. Things that happen around us and inside us daily can be studied biologically, chemically, physically and spiritually. These are just different ways to label and view the same event. The difference is only in our point of reference, isn't it?

Sometimes, events take place and there is no one to witness them and tell others what transpired or that it even happened. What occurred at the holy site of Zsa Zsa that day was not recorded in history books or even narrated as folklore. You can call it an anomaly. A blip in the Matrix. A fool's yarn. A fanatic's fable. Call it what you please. I am going to use the term 'miracle'. For me, it was a miracle. One that would have far-reaching consequences—for not only Khudir and its people but also the whole world. But, as I said, no one saw it. No one recorded it. No one studied or observed it. Maybe being observed would have changed it somehow. Maybe that's why miracles need to take place in isolation. In the quiet behind the scenes. That's what I believe, anyway.

In any case, today an infant doomed to die was saved. *Somehow.*

Divine spark.

Destiny.

Life force.

You may ask, 'Why today? Why now? Why *her*?'

And my answer is: The same reason that anything and everything happens. The same reason the grass grows. Because it is meant to. Because there is a need for it, whether we recognize it or not.

But I fear I may be digressing too much. Let us come back to our story.

On that day, the holy site of Zsa Zsa had restricted general visitors because some Very Important People were visiting. Important enough to keep the plebeians and poor citizens of Khudir from interrupting the elites' private moment of seeking blessings.

The Akhoon family. The family of Umar Akhoon. The only brother of the Great Khan.

And there you have it. Serendipity.

From chaos comes order. All in its time. Wait and watch. It will all add up ... eventually.

You see, miracles occur. But they don't come with manuals that guide you through the next steps, what must be done, what the outcome will be, and so on and so forth. You must be patient and allow things to unfold. Slowly. Like the peeling of a pungent onion. Do not be tricked by the sting of the onion tears into hastening your process. One layer will have to follow another. You cannot go faster. You have to take one step at a time. Peel one stubborn layer at a time.

The stage was now set for a chance encounter.

Umar was perhaps the only person in the world the Great Khan was patient with—perhaps the only one he even cared about. But Umar often spoke up against the atrocities committed by his brother. After many open spats, the choice was clear. Either Umar could suffer a public beheading or silent poisoning masquerading as a heart attack, O*R* he could leave with his family and live abroad, away from the affairs of the state.

The thing about royalty is that, even in exile, *royalty must always live like royalty*. A handsome annual pension and many generous perks were granted so that Umar Akhoon and his family could be in exile but continue to live in the lap of luxury. (And, much later in life, the assiduous Umar will be sipping his champagne by the cedar wood fireplace at the Ritz Carlton, minutely critiquing the despotic ways of his brother, overlooking the fact that his bottle of 1928 Krug had been paid for by money stained with the blood of his compatriots. But can you blame him for that? The champagne is *so* damn good.)

But I'm racing ahead again.

Back to that present moment of miracle.

Umar Akhoon's family had come to Zsa Zsa to seek blessings for their rather uncertain life ahead. So absorbed were they in praying for their own well-being that they failed to see the most miraculous thing happening right under their Big Fat Akhoon noses. Talk about bad luck.

A child tossed aside by the world, resurrected by the ancient holy spring and a bolt from heaven. A child who, unknown to Umar at the time, was his own blood. His elder brother's offspring. His niece.

That's the thing about paying attention, about being aware. The moment you focus on one thing, you risk missing something else. Maybe even the whole damn Big Picture.

If only the Akhoon family knew the miracle they had just missed. If only the baby knew who she was, what had touched her, how it had transformed her, what it was meant to be ... But I cannot entertain such never-ending flights of fancy, I can merely tell you what happened next.

Some distance away from where our nameless baby was bobbing to safety was parked the Akhoon family's motorcade. Many uniformed attendants hovered around Umar, his wife, Ayesha, and their brood. Security guards. A small village of attendants. Bearers carrying food in fine china on silver trays. Nannies minding the kids. An official state videographer. Makeshift luxury tents had already been set up for the family to rest in after their visit. Air-conditioned, of course.

Four kids hung around sullenly, not daring to complain about being lugged about the country, paying homage at different places of faith. In their defence, any nine-, seven-, six- and four-and-a-half-year-old would be sulking if their parents pulled them out of their beds before the crack of dawn and took them on a marathon holy pilgrimage.

The brothers – let's call them A, B, C and D – are NOT important to our story. In fact, they are so unimportant that I refuse to even give them names because they serve no purpose and too many names of irrelevant characters may confuse the reader. At best, imagine them as an overdressed, loud, spoilt background crowd. Little boys who refuse to grow up ever only because of their acute sense of entitlement which comes from their birth into money and privilege. The good thing about them was they were always available for family stuff, as we shall see later in the story.

Umar and Ayesha were leaving the country to settle in America. *Forever*. Heartbroken about their impending departure from their beloved land, they were trying to capture as much of it as they could with their handy Nikon cameras. It was 1992, and documenting daily life, particularly special occasions, like picnics, birthdays, anniversaries, park visits, holidays, random family gatherings had just started to become *en vogue*.

Umar, who fancied himself a photographer, had just got himself a new camera and was lining up his family for a beautiful photo with Zsa Zsa behind them when, suddenly, Eldest Son A spotted something.

He yelled in amazement, 'What is that?'

The baby was by now merrily bobbing in the shallow water close to the shore. She showed no sign of fear or pain or, despite being naked, that it was cold.

Eldest Son A was excited to be the first one to spot this treasure, and he raced ahead full throttle, outrunning the attendants, to wade out towards the infant. He caught the baby and, cradling her in his arms, brought her out of the water. On the shore, Nancy, the boys' head governess, took over. In a swift move, she wrapped the baby in a warm towel and gave her a quick look-over, noting her gender and counting all her toes and fingers.

Stunned by the unexpected turn of events, the family gathered around Nancy. The boys fussed and marvelled over the little cooing infant. This was surely a most exciting occurrence on an otherwise boring day. Nancy handed the baby to Ayesha for inspection, softly muttering, 'It's a girl!' so that only Ayesha could hear.

Ayesha Akhoon's face lit up. Pressing the baby gently to her chest, she looked at her husband imploringly. He sighed. Perhaps, he reasoned, some poor unwed mother had tossed the baby in the water to hide her shame. Umar shouted out to the guards, demanding to know if they had noticed anyone entering or leaving the area. This caused a small commotion, as the guards began asking each other the same question and running helter-skelter as though searching for an intruder they may have missed.

Ayesha walked towards the edge of the water. It was a beautiful dawn. The sun's rays bathed the shore. Birds chirped. The wind picked up serenely. Ayesha took a deep breath. If there was ever a peaceful sight on this planet, ***this was it***.

If there is a heaven on Earth ... it is here, it is here, it is here.

Hami asto. Hami asto. Hami asto.

She raised the baby over her head and, tears streaming down her face, said, '*Thank you! Thank you, Allah, for this miracle!*'

With that, she hugged the baby and fell to her knees, overcome with emotion. Ayesha had always yearned for a daughter, but she only had boys. She had prayed for a miracle, and finally her prayers had been answered. This child had been sent by God.

Umar looked at his wife and knew her mind was made up. He smiled. He was not a man to question faith or a woman's will. If Ayesha believed this child was sent to them by God, that her prayers had been answered by the Almighty in such a direct fashion, who was he to stand in the way?

He immediately started thinking about the next steps. First, he called his secretary and instructed him to arrange for the infant to leave Khudir along with the family. Then he walked up to his wife and put his arm around her. Ayesha rested her head on his shoulder and looked up at him. 'It has happened. He has sent us our baby girl. This is our child. My little girl,' she said in an awed whisper.

'Then we need to give our daughter a name,' Umar said simply.

'She is my Zeba. My beautiful child from Heaven.'

And just like that, in less than seventy-two hours after her birth (and very brief death), newly christened and now clad in freshly procured designer baby shoes and a Z-monogrammed baby cowl, Zeba—our newly born, freshly resurrected, future superhero blessed by ancient divine water—was being fussed over by Ayesha, Nancy and the boys. Umar walked off to smoke his cigar in peace. Grown men did not entangle themselves in all this woman–baby business, after all.

As the Akhoons' private plane took off for New York, the little Zeba screamed for her soiled wet nappy to be changed.

Zeba, the beautiful child from Heaven.

6

Inside the Mind of a Misfit

I think I'm depressed.

Okay. Mildly depressed. Early-*ish*. Borderline.

But my dumb therapist has not figured that out yet. Since I also exhibit narcissistic behaviour, I don't blame him. Plus, I'm entitled. And sometimes just plain old bratty. So, no sympathies there.

my lifestyle + sharp tongue (I call it my Rich Wit) = zero friends

Oh, I know you're judging me. Fuck off and carry on, will you? What do I care? Yes, I have rich-people issues. You know, all that 'Oh, poor me. I'm such a victim. I'm such a rebel without a cause.'

Truth be told, I'm quite charming when I choose to be. So yes, **I am an acquired taste.** Like wasabi. Not everybody likes wasabi. I don't. Even though I may be wasabi myself.

Je suis wasabi. Pungent. Effective. Dry. Sharp. Exotic. Rare.

I may be all that, but I like sweet stuff—like Bellinis. My favourite poison. Nectar of the lazy gods, especially when sipped at noon, or as a slothful sundowner. Or LIITs in those massive jars Nancy serves them in. Vodka, tequila, light rum, triple sec and a splash of cola. *Love.*

Yes, you're reading this right. I'm a day drinker.

In Busy Chaotic New York, I have what they call *The Good Life*. And all the frills and no work have made poor Zeba 'a lonely gal who goes for expensive bi-weekly therapy'. And, of course, not to forget the mandatory 'fun cultural meets and greets' with 'our people'. Kin. Relatives. In a nutshell, those folks we *have to* like and *have to* hang out with just because they look like us.

Vomit.

In general, all brown parents are a particular kind of prickly pain. My adoptive brown folks are a classic case of first-generation immigrants stuck in a certain time and place. To them, this is Khudir in the 1990s. They are forever reminiscing about the customs and traditions of their native land.

Khudir. Sounds like a make-believe place, doesn't it?

Amma–Abba. Ever since their wedding day, when Umar set eyes on Ayesha for the very first time, these two have not been apart for more than a single day. Perfect role models for arranged marriages and totally in sync with the wholly outdated gendered notion of a good masculine provider husband wedded to a caring, traditional, stay-at-home wifey. Joined in blissful matrimony.

Amma–Abba. Always together. Never apart. After relocating to America they leaned heavily on each other for comfort in this strange foreign country and were bonded deeper in their love for their beloved homeland.

Amma and Abba are like peas in a pod; nattering on about their country, the palace they lived in, the fun they had, the weddings, the parties, the friends, the *chai sessions and gup-shup*. Honestly, it's nauseating. And then the discussion over the ten thousand and one photographs they took before their sad departure from their land. More like exile. But the E-word is not allowed in the Akhoon house.

Photos and more photos ... in the palace, in the bedroom, in the great dining hall that seats six hundred people, in the kitchen, even in the damn glistening bathrooms ... They captured every inch of the glorious motherland on film, except of course the harem. No photography is allowed inside the harem. The women of the Great Khan and their boring mundane lives is a Prohibited Zone.

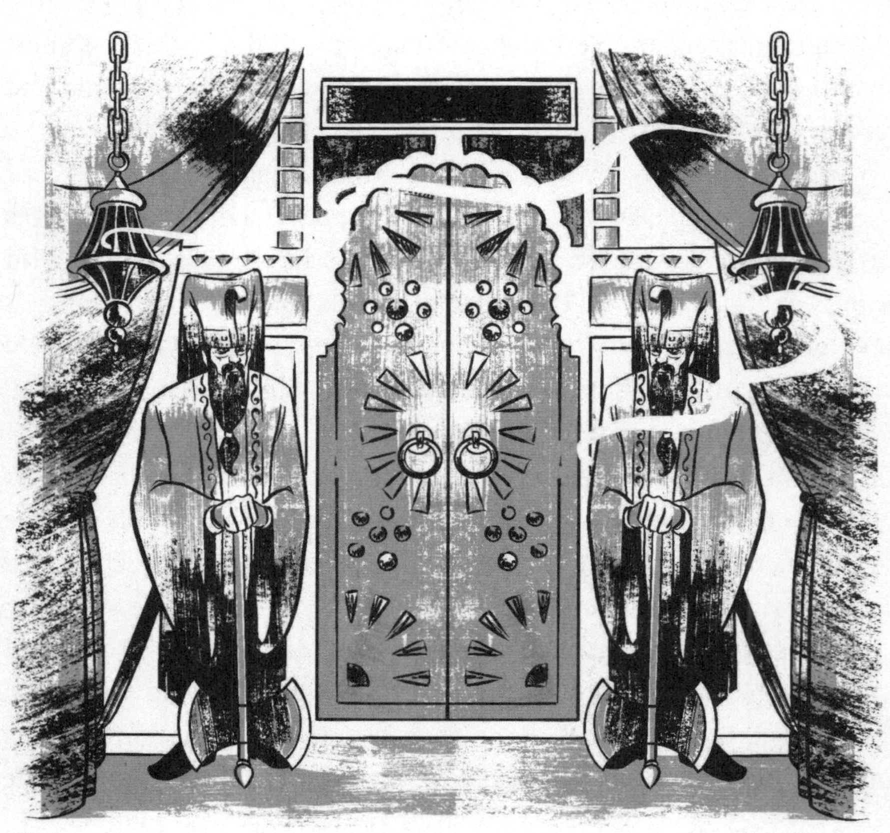

But, really, who cares about stupid photos anyway?

The only thing that can get me out of bed every day—against my self-diagnosed depressive ennui—is ... *drumroll* ... Flying planes.

And Ping-Pong. (Yes, *Forest Gump*-inspired!)

Best stuff ever.

My two loves.

Flying is so much easier than driving in Manhattan. I know you are reading this with the utmost disbelief. Put any average Joe and/or Jill inside the cockpit for the first time, and they/she/he won't be able to start the fucking engine, right? But, trust me, flying is not only much easier than driving; it is also fucking safer. I promise you.

I, for one, never wanted to learn how to drive. I refused to turn into one of those arrogant, overconfident, complacent, incompetent drivers roaring about in a vehicle with broken headlights or tail lights, or a bumper missing, mud splattered on the underside or scorch marks on the sides. Lame losers. Besides, driving needs too much attention, and attention on the freeway or narrow by-lanes is not supported by my weed habit.

Also, for anyone who feels compelled to complain about my smoking habit or my 'lack of drive'—I want to tell you losers that I passed every single flying exam. Written, oral, practical. Even earned an additional licence in radiotelephony. So, yes, whether I was smoked up and high or chomping through gummies for that FLOW state, I ploughed through my air law guides, studied my big brown ass off. Weather, aerodynamics, navigation—you name it. And I did my flying hours. And then some more.

And I can tell you one thing. It's beautiful flying up in the sky. Clean straight line. Keep going still and straight. Well, that is not always the case. But hey, I'd rather take my chances in the air than in the crazy New York traffic.

Have you ever smoked one up while flying solo?

Woo hoo! Go HIGH!

Nothing matters when you are up there in the sky looking at the world below with its narrow strips of road, boxes and lines. See everything. Do not get involved in anything. Keep going straight. Got to admit, being my Abba's kid—even though I'm adopted—does have a lot of benefits. Like his private plane. Correction. *Planes*. Plural.

Here, we have arrived at Teterboro Airport.

I spend more time here than at home. Drive in, say hello to the staff, the pilot sucking up to you, telling you how much he loves his new fiancé blah blah blah ... Teterboro. Takes more time to drive to the damn airport from New York than to fly from here to Miami. But this is the spot for folks like my family: an airport reserved for our shiny private jets. Teterboro sees more than seventy thousand departures every year, making it America's busiest airport for the sector. But that's beside the point, really.

Anyway, here it is. My love, our Gulfstream G280—a beautiful 22-million-dollar cookie. Delish. But it's nothing compared to what our distant cousin in Khudir owns. A fucking Airbus A380. That is one big motherfucker. (*Whistle whistle.*) Of course, Abba, not to be outdone, has got himself the Bombardier BD-700 Global Express, which came at a cool 40 mil, just to seat nineteen people. La family, the staff ... Everyone travelling together for our *vacay*.

Oh! Maui ... I miss your sunsets, baby.

And I must tell you about Ping-Pong. When I'm ping-ponging, it is pure bliss. Feet moving. Hand moving. Body moving. Eyes moving. In a flow. Dancing. Volleying. Love. Rhythm. I hate losing though, and have often broken my racket—and the opponent's nose on one occasion. Okay, twice. So not many people play with me now.

'Look at our first photo as a family,' Amma says, shoving the photograph at me.

The whole family and one-day-old me. All smiling, including toothless baby me. Rare smiling photo of yours truly—currently, sulky bitch.

The only thing I can think of looking at that picture is who the fuck tries to kill a day-old baby? Fucking barbarians! You don't want a baby, I get it. Use birth control. Daddy doesn't love mommy? Fine, no problem. Pull it out in time, buddy. Didn't pull out in time? Then pay for that fucking abortion, dude. Even in states where it is banned anyone can pay and find a quack. Come on, man! So *many* ways to NOT have a baby. Who the fuck goes through nine months of carrying a baby only to dispose of it in less than twenty-four hours? The growing bulge, the nausea, the agony, the crushing act of giving birth ... for what?

I mean, that is some *mind-blowingly* dumbass behaviour.

If Amma–Abba had not found me floating in the stream, if they had not saved me then ... Well, I would just be **a bundle of unwantedness at the bottom of some holy spring in that stuck-in-medieval-times kingdom**.

Did my birth mother even bother to breastfeed me? Probably not. Why feed and waste good-quality lactose on a corpse anyway?

Am I angry? Nah! How can I be angry at people with no faces, who never wanted me? Why the fuck would I care about them?

In fact, thank goodness for what they did. Otherwise, I would be growing up on some horse farm or goat farm, milking animals or whatever the fuck you do with them. Thank you for that shit. Losers.

But what do I do about Amma–Abba? They exasperate me. Always so much drama. *Natak*.

Yes, I love them. But sometimes they are just hilarious. Like the other day, I said 'Jesus' in exasperation because Nancy made my eggs super-duper dry, and Amma went on a forty-five-minute rant about how I should say 'Allah, *na*' not Jesus. Her bonny logic was that if you must take the Lord's name in vain then at least take your own Lord's name.

Arghhh. Seriously? I just wanted my scrambled eggs runny. Jesus!

Trust me, I have had to do a lot of inner work. Not about the eggs. About the attitude. I have meditated and journaled, just as my therapist told me to. But, if you ask me, it's not just a generational gap. It is a mindset gap. A cultural gap.

It doesn't matter where I was born, in my mind I am American, young(ish), or let's just say not yet thirty, and Muslim (strictly by birth). Oh yes, and I do look the way I do. Toasted brown. (Though diamonds and black athleisure, and not to forget a great blow-dry, make that brown look yummy. Lit.) And I am the living, breathing embodiment of all the confusion that comes with it. A mess. And when they force their shit on me, it makes it all worse. I have had enough kids at school making fun of our weirdness and 'other'-ness. Those mean kids can really fuck you up. Bullies at school are more lethal than nukes, dude. Despite my dad's millions, I still had to become super smart, dress sharp and be well-spoken to shut them up.

Thank God for good home-grown American weed. Hallelujah! That stuff got me through high school. And life.

Perhaps I'm still in my rebellion phase.

That's what my therapist said. My inner voice does not sound like a woman radically approaching her thirties. Instead, it still has the fuming-at-the-world angry-teenager tone and timbre. The woman who refuses to grow up and heal her hurt inner child. Stuck forever in an I-am-victim triangle.

Peter Pan. Or is it Pauline Pan?

Anyway, back to weed. It is so much fun. And fun is the most important thing in the world. Being stoned is especially great when you have created mini tornadoes in Parent Land, particularly when

@zeblah
33
Posts
768
Followers
30
Following
If I was a writer I'd have a better Instagram bio.
Follow
Message

my folks are lecturing me on what to do and how to run my life: get married, stop being eccentric, have some ambition, don't dismiss your overpaid security detail ...

Like that time when Abba was in form. 'I am a mo-derrrrn man. I want to give you all a gooood life. But you have to be more rrespoonsible,' he had said in his heavily accented grainy voice. My father, who always dresses impeccably even at home. Not a hair out of place. Sitting back in his favourite chair, like an old oil painting. Portrait of a Gentleman.

'Zeba, do you know with great powerrrr'—*OMG! Is Abba going to quote Stan Lee to me?*—'comes great humility.'

I sniggered. Of course, a native twist.

Humility. Respect. *Adab*.

Iqhlaaq. Good speech.

Trust Abba-jaan to misquote the most famous movie line ever.

I often wonder how he gets by in life. Living in his bubble. Expecting his kids to float in similar bubbles. Or live a pretend life. Our real lives are very different from our Instagram lives. No social media 'fun' pictures, because 'You know which family you belong to.' We may not be in line for the throne but 'Never forget your roots. You are a princess of Khudir.'

Bullshit! I'm just some unwanted embryo that some peasant in Khudir should've had the *good akal* to abort in time.

A pretend princess at best. I mean, what dismal luck. I could just burst out crying.

But hey, wait a minute, I forgot to tell you how big a freak I really am. *I have never cried*. Of course, I've felt hurt and upset, but no tears have ever formed in or flowed from my eyes. It has baffled Amma–Abba ever since they found me. It baffled poor Reggie in Grade Six when he slashed my thumb with his pencil knife. It baffled all my therapists and physicians. But it did not baffle me. To me, the writing was always on the wall. I am a weirdo. I totally accept that.

Don't those spiritualists say something about acceptance and surrender? I went to a chanting group once. Focus on a flickering flame. Open your heart chakra. It was okay, but I find these things too cult-y. Don't shoot me!

But I digress yet again. My point is, why fight it? We always know who we are, what we are made up of. I for one am acutely aware. But my Muslim parents with their pots of money had not heard of this acceptance spiel. They had to fix it. So, years of doctor consultations and many tests later, it was finally deduced that Zeba had 'non-functioning tear glands'. Medical science had spoken.

Applause.

Honestly, I think it's pretty cool. Not crying makes me look braver than I am. Stronger than I am. No boy can bully me. And no fucking soppy movie date can melt me. No tears. No fears.

The only time it becomes a bit uncomfortable is at funerals. I hate funerals and weddings in any case. Basically, I detest any place where you have a gathering of more than six over-excited, frenzied, lively, energetic, overtly happy or sad people. People give me anxiety. Unless it is a concert. But that's another trip altogether.

Today, the family gathered post lunch. Abba smoked his cigar, while Amma carried on about some wedding, a party, a trip.

To Khudir.

Really?

I protested. I didn't want to be part of some decadent Aladdin party in the middle of nowhere ... where good dollars are being wasted on exotic four-humped camels and shish kebabs.

We argued for thirty minutes, during which my parents proved (yet again) that they are always right. My mother is not an easy adversary. Her arsenal is full of emotional manipulation, and unlike me she has no problem shedding tears. She always has the final word. The woman loves her mic drop finales.

So it will be as Ammi has decided. A trip for my cousin's wedding—a cousin whom I've never met or spoken to, not even on the phone. Desert kingdom it is. To meet my extended family. Dance to tribal music. Meet my paternal uncle who is a fucking king. A dictator. *Jesus!* Er, I mean, Allah. (Better start practising taking my own Lord's name already.)

The kebabs better be worth the trip.

7

The Great Khan

Bad boys ain't no good.
Good boys ain't no fun.

My back hurts. The heat of the hammam should help, the Royal Doctor said. I did not object. I like spending my afternoons at the hammam. I had mine built almost fifteen years ago.

Two attendants are buzzing around me like flies, soaping me up and scraping me with that rough towel. Detoxification indeed. The heat is rising. I want all of them to leave me alone and let me sleep on my marble bed for a bit. The marble floor and gold faucets gleam so much I can see my face in them.

Today, the women have not joined me. I like their company, especially when they shed their clothes, but today I want some stillness. They chatter too much, always trying to get my attention. Silly women.

One peasant girl I had with me for nineteen months told me it was worth being my concubine because it allowed her to use this beautiful hammam and indulge herself. They do not have water in her village, it seems. She was a beautiful one. Lovely grey eyes. Spoke too much but had such a beautiful ass. Sadly, she did not last long.

I can feel the masseur's palms press down on my shoulder blades. I hold all my stress and tension between my shoulder blades, he says. His firm hands feel good. Today should have been my day of rest. But the new US ambassador is scheduled to visit. He is desperate for a better trade route through Khudir. Desperate for better oil prices. He is coming all the way to ... er... what is that term ... to *kiss the ring. Kiss my ring.*

My motherland. My Khudir. Strategically placed between India, Pakistan, China and Afghanistan, high up in the mountains and *oil rich.* Sounds too good to be true, does it not?

It did, until I made it happen. Through my powers. I shall never forget that day, 8 April 1988. The day I found ... nay, *made* oil appear in Khudir. The day that changed everything forever for this land. The rise of the ***Greatest Tiniest Nation on Earth*** and of its Great Khan!

I am no ordinary King. My powers are beyond political, diplomatic, constitutional or electoral. My powers are of the other world.

I can do anything.

Anything.

We were once a country crushed and shoved around like a ragged football between global giants. But I made them all toe the line. I recognized the true power of Khudir and stood up to those assholes. I told them *my terms.* I love these negotiations—where my power is evident, where the balance is titled in *my* favour.

The masseur works rigorously on my back. I feel the full extent of the stiffness in my muscles plagued by stress knots. A small groan escapes my lips, and he jumps aside in fear. Bubbles of mirth rise from my stomach and escape my lips in a gleeful snort.

I love the effect I have on people. I'm sure it's how Hollywood movie stars feel. Everybody watches you closely, in anticipation of the next royal fit. Hanging on to every word, every little whim that escapes your lips. But I am more than some Tom Cruise or Brad Pitt. I can have *everything* I want. I can pay to watch *them* dance.

I am King.

Of course, it is tough business. Being a *dictator*. Not a word anyone will dare use in my presence. Even in private they say it in hushed whispers. In public they call me The Khan or The Great Khan. I like that. It's friendly and nice. 'Dictator' has got too much bad press throughout history.

One day, I'm going to write a book about it. What shall I call it?

A Dictator's Handbook? An Oppressor's Manual? Scent of a Despot?

Ha ha ha!

I raise my head to catch my breath and see my reflection in the small hanging mirror. The forehead Botox and undereye fillers need a touch-up. Must call in Dr Simon before the guests arrive. A little prickly prick and the years will melt away. Just in time for my son's, my dear Bassam's, wedding, too.

I ring for the attendants to come in and dress me. And perfume me and powder me. They arrive promptly and lead me to my changing suites. I enjoy watching them fuss over me now.

For so many years, I have ruled this great land and lived life on my terms. Travelled the world. Shook hands with all those proud prime ministers and presidents—all trying to woo me for my oil reserves. The seasonal faggots have changed over the years, but a King is a King. This is why I have always liked the old Queen in London: she and I share a kinship. A bond. The king of a nearby kingdom had often been a guest at Khudir. But then there was some drama about a deranged family member walking in and shooting down the whole royal family. And the kingdom became a democracy. Sad business.

I will never let something like that happen in Khudir. Democracy? Elections? Over my dead body.

Khudir is special. An unbroken line of Akhoons has ruled this land, and today Khudir has become a power player. It is going to remain this way. I will ensure that both Khudir and I, as King of Khudir, stay in power—for eternity.

Our older tribal kings did not have much political clout; they were often terrorized by our mighty neighbours. Until I, the Great Khan, got those losers to behave. *Me*. I am the First Great True Leader this land has ever seen. I brought peace to this land. And power. And power is everything.

Whatever the people say, I'm not some crazy monster chopping up my enemies and feeding them to unassuming guests in some royal banquet. That would be *haraam*. I'm not like that crazy Bokassa. Or Idi Amin. I'm not a beast. I just feed traitors to hungry wild cats.

If you want to really know a man, see what's on his plate. I stand by these words. My chefs can tell you who I am *and* how much I love food—lamb meat, meatballs with rice, soupy with red gravy. And I love peaches. I have them specially flown in from Afghanistan. My head chef, Rasul, knows how to make a lovely peach murabba.

Oh! I love my food and I love my chefs, especially my head chef, Rasul. Such a delicate hand he has with spices—cardamom, saunf (what an exquisite spice!), saffron, dry red chillies (the one with a strong after-kick), and garlic. I love it when he roasts whole garlic over hot coals or in a tandoor to serve with my desi chicken, marinated the entire night in spices especially imported from India.

My breakfast is always the same: Breads. Salted butter. Salted tea. Unless Rasul has lovingly kept some murabba or lavender honey to be devoured early in the morning. I swear my day is so much better if I start it with perfectly spiced peach murabba.

My chefs have learnt to always keep a fabulous meal ready for me after I've had a hard day at work. They know that an empty belly makes me feel murderous. Oh, how they all shudder. Except Rasul. He understands me and always has a treat ready for me when I return from some skirmish. He knows I hate being in a terrible mood. That I make bad decisions when I'm hungry.

Rasul was born in a small village a few miles from where I was born, so he knows all the dishes of my childhood—mutton stew with potatoes; fried freshwater fish in gravy with grilled juicy chunky tomatoes; haak, that delicious form of spinach; nadru or lotus steam; cheese made from yak's milk; and grilled gucchee (what a rare mushroom!). Over the years, Rasul has also picked up dishes from all over the world. His shepherd's pie is better than the one made at Buckingham Palace. I know this because I had once requested to eat it there, and it was not half as good as Rasul's. I especially telephoned home to tell him this. I'm sure the bloody spying white royals thought it was a coded message.

Now that Bassam's wedding is approaching, Rasul's skills will be put to the test. We must make the celebrations as glorious as possible.

My son, my heir, deserves a royal wedding that the world will talk about for years to come.

Ah, my son! Bassam, the jewel of my eye, has appointed a whole team just to ensure that all our produce is obtained from 'friendly farms' or brought in from around the world. He even put together a team of food tasters to ensure that all the food that reaches me has been tasted and declared safe forty-five minutes before I am supposed to eat it. Not without reason.

Bassam, my blessed boy, put in place this extra precaution ever since we discovered that our last head chef, Mirotkshi, was a Japanese spy. We had to execute him, of course. A tragedy really! His unagi roll and rice pudding were such a delight. That's why I had him prepare a last meal for me—his last, not mine—before we shot him dead. It may have been made at gunpoint, but it was perfection. He did not let his fear seep into the meal. What a master.

Since then, all my food is tasted before it comes anywhere near me. Just as well. It would be a shame if I died ingloriously of poisoning. The Great Khan, slain by the hand of a mere cook. Eyes bulging. Mouth frothing. And then, suddenly, my head falling smack into my goulash or curry. Such a pity that kind of death would be. Unacceptable.

The women finish dressing me, and I lie down on the bed and look at the feroza-studded ceiling with an intricate geometric pattern all over it. I am trying to think about my guest list, but I am preoccupied by a certain nostalgia today.

Weddings and funerals are sentimental occasions: the start of a new life, the end of another. Makes one emotional just thinking about them. I should know. I've been married six times—officially, that is. Which means that six of my wives have found a place in the *Royal Book of Wedding Alliances*. The others, well ... let's just say the expense and time consumed did not make sense to make them official.

Bassam's mother. She was my first wife. A lovely woman. The daughter of the last Nizam of Oudhabad. To be honest, that did not mean much, considering the Nizams had long been stripped of their titles by the Government of India. All that remained for them to enjoy were some standalone palace properties and a measly pension. Most of their family heirlooms had found a place in government-run museums and their palaces slowly converted into exotic hotels. Silly. Still, blood is blood and royal blood is rarer than peacock egg-sized emeralds.

I believe in the power of blood and lineage. It is something no amount of money can buy, no democratic government can suppress. People will more often look at the lineage of a horse or dog before they buy them, but not of their wives. How idiotic. That's a woman who will make heirs for you. You have to know where she comes from.

So yes, I am excited about my eldest son's wedding. It has been a while since Khudir saw a big celebration. My last wedding was three years ago. Since then, we have not had any reason to celebrate. And I did not have my whole family with me. My brother did not join us. In fact, he has not come back to the country since he left in 1992.

Fool. I did not even banish him. I do not believe in banishment. Execution is better. Less messy. If I started banishing everyone who disagreed with me, do you know what a mess that would create?

But this invitation ... this one my brother has accepted. I am happy. Very happy. I love my brother. I do. This wedding has got me so excited. It is going to bring us all together. Such a silly fight we had years ago over some random shooting of villagers. I do not even remember the details. Now all our fights and bitterness will be forgotten. Umar and I will break bread together, drink some lovely vintage wine, and I will show him our newly refurbished palace and some carefully curated parts of the country. It will be so special. I cannot wait.

Umar seems happy in his new American life. I know because I keep a close eye on him. I have so many enemies, and I hate to have a weakness. It actually costs me more to keep him alive in America than in Khudir. But I must admit, he has good taste! Especially that last gold Ferrari he purchased. Beautiful! I got one just like that too. Every time I look at the weekly dossier full of his pictures and bank statements, I am reminded of our childhood. The bittersweet memories. Even though his mother was a bitch to me, Umar will always be my brother. My father's son. My blood. Our youngest. The last of the Akhoons. Along with me of course.

Zahid the Benevolent was our Baba, the leader of our tribe. His kindness was the stuff of legend. He was the first to unite the warring tribes of our small country under his leadership. One Clan of All

Khudirs! He introduced the idea of One Nation One People to the fragmented tribes without ever going to war, without once raising his weapon. Silly man, it took him twenty years to do what one year of terror would have achieved. His head was filled with stupid notions of non-violence and empathy. But I cannot change a dead man's life choices now, can I?

But I loved my father. I still do. Zahid the Benevolent. The First of the Akhoons.

We Akhoons are a proud people who have ruled over Khudir since the time it was just rubble. Just stones and mountains. Goatherds and soothsayers. Our true might came from our knowledge both of the real tangible world and the hidden secrets of the spirit world. We knew many of its mysteries. We knew, most importantly, how to harness black magic and its true potential. Yet, the Akhoons, including my father, Zahid the Benevolent, were a dumb lot, happy with what they had. They never learnt how to protect themselves or use the power of this magic. They had vowed to never use it to harm anyone. Not even an ant. They wanted to use it to benefit humanity.

Fools. Idealists. You cannot have that kind of power and remain on the sidelines.

But Umar does not know this. I have never told him the story. *Our story.* Of how he could have almost been King.

When I was younger, I feared it would corrupt him. Make him want to fight me. Fight for power. Fight for the throne. He was just a baby when it all happened. And as he grew up, it became clear that he did not care to be King. That's why he is so happy with his cushy life in America doing American things. No, Umar would never think of moving back here. So now I know that it is safe to tell him the truth. That he is our father's last legitimate son. Because Baba never actually married my mother even though she was the love of his life and he had five children with her. And he did not give me his name. Not until he had to—on his deathbed. Not until he realized that none of my elder brothers were alive. Had Baba died without giving me his name, it would be Umar on the throne. Not me—the bastard son of Zahid the Benevolent.

Umar was such a child then. He would not remember what happened. But I do. The way he clung to my arm when they bombed us. I took care of him. I protected him. I will protect him always. I never left him wanting for anything. He was all I had left. And I was all he had. We had to take care of each other. Everyone else had been wiped out, our entire village. Leaving behind only four-year-old Umar, Baba, who was barely alive, and me.

The sound of baby Umar's voice calling out to me—'Bhai! Bhai!'—rings in my ears. The memories come flooding back. How he screamed and held on to me. How he sought my protection. The first person in my life who taught me to be stronger than I was, braver than I was. For that, I can never repay him. He made me King before I was crowned.

I pull myself away from the bed, a sense of impatience building inside. I cannot wait for Umar to get here so I can finally tell him the whole story.

I want to hug you when I see you, my jaan.
And tell you our story.

8

New Lust and Old Hate

Who knew that when our jet touched down stylishly in Khudir, love would be waiting for me as I emerged in my new custom-made Balenciaga airport PJ set, lugging a whining Doobie in a silver cage from the house of Cartier behind me?

Correction. Lust. Not Love. Not so soon anyway.

If someone had told me when I was boarding the plane to Khudir that this trip would be so eventful ... that I would meet the man of my dreams *and* become sworn enemies with my Uncle Khan, I would have laughed. Not a full-blown hearty laugh. Just the condescending, incredulous kind. But here I am, thinking carnal, kinky thoughts while ogling at the love-slash-lust of my life. Sigh ...

Uh-oh, and ... YUCK! I sound like one of those lovestruck girls who only dream of romance, marriage and their Prince Charming. I may not know what I want to do with my troubled life, but I'm certainly not waiting for some man to sweep me off my feet.

Anyway, we are at a lavish dinner at my Uncle Khan's palace when I first notice *his* butt. But(t), obviously. And what a work of art it is! I let my eyes and ears take in a little more as I pretend to focus on the obscene spread of edibles before me. His manners are raw. His speech full of one-liners designed to both shock you and reel you in. He sits there in a luxe tux, fidgeting in a way that makes him inelegantly sexy. I can just picture him in an old, stained T-shirt, chilling all day, feet up, smoking up with me, laughing at people and watching dumb TV shows.

You know that moment when you look at a person and instantly know that one day your nose will be less than six inches away from his? That you will lick chocolate off his chin? That your bodies will entwine and move rhythmically and in perfect harmony? That feeling of having been someplace before, a familiarity? As if a magnetic pull is drawing you in, until inevitably one day your lips have no option but to be locked passionately with his? I've had that feeling at least twelve times before. And I have always been right.

Turns out, the cutest butt is attached to an actor from India. A superstar. A heartthrob of millions. My uncle has a thing for hobnobbing with movie stars, it seems. Hmm. Good For Me. Danke, King Khan. And cheers to your heavy appetite for movie stars, botched-up facial fillers and nauseating quantities of fattening calorie-laden food. You are quite the lardy freak show.

As I sit here, at this illustrious table, *I know that he knows that I know* that he is feeling as much an imposter as I am. He is playing a part, just the way I am. A character straight out of a Hindi musical.

No. It is not love at first sight. But it is *something*. We look at each other. One imposter at another. It is a relief to spot a kindred soul among a sea of people. Someone as uncomfortable as you are. Someone waiting just as impatiently to break the rules. As I chew on my kale salad and survey his body, he suddenly looks at me and smiles. Ah! He has such a good-boy attitude with a bad-boy vibe. I smile back but only with my eyes. I must tease him a little.

I shift some of my focus back to the food. The cod is simply divine. Or perhaps everything just *seems* heavenly. Lust can be such a magical thing. It makes banal days and boring dinners seem infinitely more fun. Mr Bollywood, it seems, is lactose intolerant. Or vegan. Or perhaps both. But eats carbs like a motherfucker. Mmm. Dishy. Under normal circumstances, I could never imagine myself falling for some Bollywood type. But this guy is kind of a misfit. I can make an exception this time around, I tell myself.

'Olive cake?' the server interrupts my sensual thoughts.

'No, thanks. I have to fit into my dress!' I reply, mentally undressing Mr Bollywood.

RK. They call him RK. Our server gives me a fake-polite smile, probably reserved for guests he must serve but cannot stand, and quietly moves on.

'She has quite the spunk. Your *adopted one*!' the Great Khan says to my father.

My uncle always speaks like he has a massive rod stuck up his ass and it will slip out if he smiles or laughs or coughs or speaks like a normal person. And he *neverrrrr everrrrr* speaks to me directly. I've realized that when he looks at me, he has the disappointed look of a buyer who has been conned into buying something overpriced, tasteless and tacky. Maybe it is just me and my blunt Amreekan-ness. But, to be honest, I have never seen him speak directly to any woman. It's almost as if it is beneath him to address anyone who possesses female genitalia.

She has quite the spunk. Your adopted one! The words have been burnt into my mind now. If you want to say something, say it to me. *Asshole.*

I smile demurely. If I were twelve, I would have stuck my tongue out at the old fogey. 'New Yorkers are known for their spice, not sugar, Uncle,' I say. 'You should get outta this spot and visit us in the First World.'

'Spunk *and* cheek. *Badtameezi* is not a good thing in a woman. It seems that your mother didn't teach you that.' The Great Khan gives me a cold hard stare. Long. Disapproving. Urging me to retort.

My brothers A, B, C and D have stopped chewing.

They are all so old now but, alas, not a wee bit wise and as useless as they were when they were little. Fresh off the plane, all they wanted was to stuff their faces and get aromatherapy massages. I didn't expect for a second that any of them would step in or even try and mitigate the situation. Despite being in America, they still lived in my parents' home and looked like leeches in tailored suits. I stayed far, far away from them.

Abba doesn't notice the tension as he is busy trying to eat his corn on a cob in a dignified manner. I don't even know how that is possible. *Abba! Just go for it and stop trying to be civil about it,* I want to scream. Back home, Amma would have said something, but she has barely uttered a word since we got here. Stunned into patriarchal silence by the presence of this alpha ruler, I suppose. The other random/famous guests also stop eating and joking, unnerved.

Pin-drop silence descends.

My uncle and I are stuck in a stare. A smiling eye-lock. I know he is baiting me. I show immense restraint, despite my temperament. I know he is eager to throw my insolent ass to his tigers. And I do not want to die yet. Still, I cannot look away. We hold each other's gaze, refusing to back down. Each hating on the other immensely, for their mere presence and existence in this world.

Little did Zeba know at that time that their dislike for each other was not new but forged the moment she was conceived. This was not a case of hating toxic patriarchy or horrid dictators but something much more. Something Zeba felt in her bones but did not fully comprehend. Often, truths don't reveal themselves until much later in the story.

I hear my father gently clearing his throat to break the impasse. The Khan's shoulder gives the slightest twitch. He has heard it too. But neither of us look away.

That is a strange, complicated relationship—the one between Abba and Uncle Khan. *Love. Hate. Gratitude. Debt. Jealousy.* God fucking knows what it is.

After we had landed at the Khan International Private Airport in Khudir, in the motorcade, on our way to the palace, Abba told the driver to take a short detour and stop by The Square. After a moment's hesitation, the driver turned the car. In a short while, we came to a roundabout. Quite green and very empty, with a massive hoarding looming overhead that had some words scrawled across it. I squinted my eyes to read it.

The Khan is your King and Father. He will always watch over you.

Hmm ... 'watch over you'? Sounded more like a threat than a public service ad.

Abba had asked for the car to be stopped. He looked at the hoarding and I thought I heard him sigh. Then he extended his hands, uttered a prayer and blew the prayer into the wind. Turning to the driver, he asked him to continue to the palace. I made a mental note to ask Abba later about this spot, but I didn't get around to ...

Sorry, just digressed, didn't I? Dammit!

Let me rewind. Back to the present moment—the face-off ...

So here I was, happily lusting after RK, when the Khan decided to get snide with me.

Stare. Stare. Unhealthy silence. Neither party willing to back down despite Abba's mild attempts at distraction.

The Khan's nostrils are now starting to flare, yet the smile remains plastered on his face—a sick, blatantly false smile, making him look a

بسم الله الرحمن الرحيم
THE KHAN IS
YOUR KING AND FATHER.
HE WILL ALWAYS
WATCH OVER YOU.

little loony. I wonder if I should stick my tongue out as a personal act of defiance, but scenes of death and execution float breezily before my eyes. Honestly, adult decisions are so hard.

CLANK! THUD!

The death stare between us breaks at the sound of a dish falling. RK has knocked over the jug of maple syrup. The *almost* murderous moment is gone. Diffused. I smile, take a sip of my wine. *Another reason to like this filmy dude,* I think. The clumsy klutzy knight in shining armour with dreamy eyes and a killer smile.

To give credit where credit is due: The Khan certainly does things in style. From the VVVVIP Dreamliner with a high-domed ceiling, hardwood floors, sculpted doors and soft Persian carpets with silk accents to the special menu—Michelin-star level, of course—consisting of all our favourite dishes and taking care of our preferences and allergies: no tomatoes, refined flour and sugar for me; no shellfish for Abba; organic vegetables and lamb stew for Ammi; beef steak and salad for Brother A; Mac and cheese with banoffee pie for Brother B; truffle fries and Dr Pepper for Brother C. Hell, it seems like he even figured out how much salt each of us likes in our food. Khudir's intelligence service would put the CIA to shame, dude. Brother D was on his sixteen-hour IF and was guzzling pots of black coffee and sparkling water.

The coolest thing though was that instead of boarding passes, we were handed customized gold tablets by the flight attendants. These tablets controlled everything, from the lights and the video and audio monitors to the window shades. The monitors displayed detailed itineraries for our two-week visit, complete with menus for each meal and a map of the palace grounds so we wouldn't lose our way (or wander into places we're not meant to be in). We also got some kind of smartwatches called FitBit to track our fitness levels, body temperatures, heart rate and oxygen levels. My tablet had a folder with pictures of all the wedding outfits that I could choose from, already custom-made, and a profile of the team selected to do my hair and make-up. They had done the winning Miss World's make-up the previous year.

I rolled my eyes. Clearly, the Khudir intelligence service did not know me THAT well.

I spent the entire plane journey trying to pull my satin LV eye mask over my eyes and pretending to sleep. But who was I kidding? It was a seventeen-hour flight. I had to get up at some point and walk around, stretch, pee.

At one point, when I got up to use the bathroom, I caught Brother B munching on crisps and watching a special video made for the wedding, playing as part of the *in-flight entertainment*.

It was a nightmare. The eyesore of a video played excruciating details about the ***Preparations for the Royal Wedding***. Themes, venues, clothes, jewellery ... everything. Watching it was as painful as the pus-filled pimple on my chin brought on every month by my mild-but-now-in-control PCOS-related symptoms. I immediately thought of calling Netflix and tipping them off to pitch for the rights to this monstrosity. Might sell for millions. Everyone wants to watch rich people do weird 'rich people' shit.

The Royal Wedding is going to be no joke. The Khan has clearly planned for his first-born Bassam's wedding to be the most extravagant and debauched party imaginable. No expense is going to be spared.

A slew of celebrities has been invited to attend. Mrs Clinton, Ivanka and Michelle Obama from my side of the world. On different days of course. One has confirmed her presence at the *sangeet* (a musical party night). One at the wedding day. And one at the reception. And then Shah Rukh Khan, Chris Hemsworth, Charlize Theron, Zendaya and Leo De Caprio, to name drop a few. There were many others, but these are the few names I could remember.

Beyonce and Elton John are rumoured to have agreed to perform on one of the evenings. Billie Eilish is coming for sure. The bride, a wealthy Indian princess, is a fan apparently. And a bunch of who's who from Hollywood and Bollywood will be flown in. All expenses paid—all seven days.

The most expensive pink champagne will be poured and chefs from over twenty-two countries will prepare the most impeccable wedding dishes. Fireworks and performances galore. It promises to be an extravaganza of a lifetime.

I buzz my attendant to get me a Xanax. I wonder how neon hair will look on me as I put on my headphones to drown out nauseous thoughts.

All the good girls go to Hell.
'Cause even God herself has enemies.

9

My Gherkin, My Jaan

I must protect her.

I knew this the moment I held the little bundle in my arms. My little Zeba. Stubborn as a wild steed. Calm and cool as a mini cucumber. And acidic like ... What are those called—the yummy, pickled ones? Ah ... Gherkins. Yes, she is my adorable little gherkin.

Every day, I watch as my brave child navigates a roller coaster of emotions. Her inner battles, monsters, demons. She smiles and sulks. Acts impudent. Acts immature. Brushes aside her fears with a toss of her hair as if they are not real things, just figments of her imagination. But her pain, her emptiness ... It is all real. I know this because I am her mother.

She may not be born of my flesh, but she is born from my heart. I know her heartbeat. I know her smell. Her moods. Her imagination. Her darkness. Her sarcasm. Her mental chatter. Her anger. Her boredom. Children often give such little credit (or none at all) to parents ... thinking we do not truly understand them.

Often, I mask my knowledge, my understanding of her. And she hides her inner world, her pain and angst in pure rebellion, behind a facade of arrogance. I do not know what life has in store for her. But

I know she is a special one, my Zeba. Perhaps all mothers think that way about their children. Do they not?

I look out at my boys trying to fly drones in the massive palatial gardens and shake my head. My stupid boys and their toys. I admit, they are all grown men, but for me they will always be my little boys. And perhaps in many ways they do not behave any older than pimply, spoilt teenagers. Love them as I do, they are idiots.

Any mother will tell you that one cannot choose between one's children. But secretly we do have our favourites. I would deny it if anyone ever quoted me on this, but I too have my special one. My Zeba, my gherkin, my jaan ... born of my heart.

Oh, but how she annoys me. Drives me insane, that girl. Is it possible to love someone this much and be absolutely exasperated with them at the same time? And Allah, does she love a fight! Nostrils flaring, eyes blazing. Ready to fly off the handle at the slightest provocation. And she seems to have somehow acquired that sharp Akhoon tongue. Allah! Thank God for her medicinal weed. Yes, I have known about this little habit of hers for years. Children rarely appreciate a mother's instinct. Initially I was worried about her becoming an addict but it is actually doing her some good. Calms her down. Cools her mind. My consultation with Dr Singh, her therapist, gave me some insight into this. Anything to keep her sanity and my peace intact. And thanks to her, I enjoy my CBD gummies. I find them so very relaxing. They give me relief from the aches of old age.

It is hard to make children understand the value of legacy, of where they really come from, who they are. By the time they exit their childhood rebellion phase and head to teenage angst and then tumble into the turbulence of the twenties, a lot of time is lost. And along with that, a lot of history too. Memories erased, people dead, recipes forgotten, letters lost, tastes disremembered, fragrance evaporated.

Fanaah. Lost. Gone. Forever.

Legacy.

That is all that matters, is it not? Now, in the menopausal phase of my life, having lived and seen it all—through my hot flashes, irritability, nutritional supplements and night sweats—I realize that legacy is all that matters, all that helps us navigate life. Where we come from enables us to take better decisions about where we are headed.

But how does one explain this to children? The boys will not understand. And Zeba will not listen. I suppose sooner or later it will come to her as a realization, that life is not a battle. Between the past and present, tradition and modernity. It is all the same. The same unbroken chain of existence. Even though it feels ruptured, there exists a continuum.

My Zeba. She is a gorgeous child, but she cannot be taught anything. She must learn on her own. Make her own mistakes. Fall and hurt her knees. Skin her shins. Till then, we fight. She resists. I persist. It is a game both of us enjoy. She argues with us but always gives in. Always comes around. Stubbornly, sullenly—but she does. She cares for and loves us more than she would want to admit.

I say a prayer of *shukran* for my child and sit back to enjoy my tea made with cinnamon and saffron, and not contaminated with milk. I chew on a little Khudiri biscuit. How I've missed these little baked local goodies.

Bang!

Allah! What has happened?

A drone has crashed into the gate; another one lies forlorn in the fountain. I sigh and focus on my tea and biscuit.

Later in the day, we are headed to Zsa Zsa for our pilgrimage.

I know it is going to be hard for Zeba to visit the place where she was abandoned, where she was left to die. This is the first time she will be visiting the site. Zeba has never shied away from abusing the circumstances of her birth and adoption. So this trip is very important. I know it will not be easy, but Dr Singh felt it would be a major milestone for her. A catharsis that might help her come to terms with her past. Perhaps, it is better that the boys and Umar have decided to stay back. My Zeba will need some time on her own to process it. I, of course, will be by her side, to hold her in case the need arises.

During the drive to Zsa Zsa, she is unusually quiet. I try to break the silence several times. But she is gloomy. In all fairness, I am distracted as well. The Great Khan has been noticing Zeba's insolence. I detest the man, but he has to be shown some reverence even if for a few days, since we are his guests.

I cautiously bring up the subject. 'You must be nice to Uncle Khan. He is taking such good care of us.'

'You mean he has been a big annoying show-off?'

'Khan Saab does not need to impress his own brother's family.'

'Well, you should tell *him* that. And he needs to stop squashing us with his rules and timetables. He is a bully and a bore.'

'Zeba! How rude ... you cannot ...'

'Or what? He will use his dark magic and turn me into a pumpkin?'

I gasp. 'How do you ...?'

'Oh Amma! That's hardly a secret now, is it? I noticed *that ugly shawl* the day we arrived. He was wearing it when he received us.' She turns to the chauffeur. 'Right, Riyaz?'

I am speechless. Such loose talk about important matters could cost us. But who can stop Zeba once she has started. 'That Chaddor that is supposedly the symbol of his dark powers looks quite plain, to be honest. A little tattered, really.'

Keep your cool, Ayesha. *Control. Breathe.*

'Yes,' I say quietly, 'it is old. Many moons ago, around the time your father and I left the kingdom ... That is when he obtained the Chaddor.'

Silence.

'Zeba, love, you have to be careful.'

'Why? Because the driver could be a spy?' Zeba whispers in a mock-serious voice, then throws her head back and laughs uproariously. 'So typical, Amma.'

Allah, there is no stopping this girl!

'Uncle Khan is a sorcerer and has used his dark magic to unlock this ancient cave. And now he is the possessor of this Cloak of Light, his Chaddor. It gives him immense power, beyond anyone in the world. Right?'

I maintain a stunned silence. How does she know all this?

Zeba laughs and winks at Riyaz.

I see. Now it makes sense. Riyaz has been Zeba's shadow from the moment we landed in Khudir. He was sent to pick us up in a shiny Phantom Rolls Royce, and he played a song that Zeba and he seemed to bond over. Some rubbish hip-hop song about sex.

'Riyaz has been kind enough to update me on our history and the Great Khan's magical powers.'

Riyaz turns around and gives me a sheepish smile.

'Riyaz wants to go to Amreeka with us—the promised land. The King is not very open and inclusive, it seems. Not a safe country, this. Especially for gay people. Kyun, Riyaz?'

Riyaz smiles coquettishly.

My heart almost gives out. This girl is such a troublemaker. Riyaz could be executed for such public declarations.

Riyaz clears his throat. 'I would love to discover the rich history of the land and its people. Amreeka. Must be so *free*, ma'am. I want to live freely and openly, without any fear.'

'Stop this, both of you. Riyaz, you should know better. Zeba, your uncle is a powerful man. Very powerful. These are not matters to be joked about.'

Riyaz clears his throat again. 'Madam is right, Zeba bi. Legend has it that when the evil force of Yazoo rises and attacks Earth, only the person who possesses the Chaddor will be able to lead and defend its people. The Chaddor controls everything on this Earth created by Allah. It controls Yazoo, the greatest evil force known to humanity. The Yazoo is resting now, dormant. But the Khan owns the Chaddor, and it is only a matter of time before he controls Yazoo too.'

'So what is Uncle Khan waiting for?'

'That, I do not know. But here is what I do know: Since the Great Khan unsealed that cave and obtained the Chaddor, he has left no opportunity to flaunt its ownership. He walks around with it hanging on his shoulders during important public occasions and ceremonies. People fear him even more because of it. To you, bi, it may look like a mere tribal shawl with geometric patterns. For us, in Khudir, it is the ultimate symbol of power. The Khan is the most important man in the world. No doubt about that.'

Zeba is listening with attention and I am relieved. At least, Riyaz is talking some sense into her. The Khan is not to be messed with. He is no ordinary King. He has found a way to tap into ancient Akhoon magic. Just then Zeba blows out her bubblegum till it bursts. A true-blue millennial. Stretching with a yawn, she says, 'It's a great story. But I'm bored. Do we have any snacks?'

'Zeba!'

'What? I don't care for this place, this fucking misogynist King or how powerful he is. Whether he is a magician or has access to some ancient black magic or the sun shines out of his ass, I don't give a shit. I'm here coz you wanted me to be here. I will attend this stupid wedding, and then I will go home. I want no part in it beyond that. One week later, I will be at home and all this will be a bad dream that I should not have been forced to participate in in the first place.'

'Zeba, please!'

'Mom. I know you believe in these stories. I don't want you to stop believing them. Please go ahead. Make it the gospel truth of your life. But don't push me. I will not believe in this rubbish. I will not even give it lip service. I cannot. It's too silly. It's honestly laughable. You guys are out of your minds.'

With that, she turns to the window and sullenly stares out of it, and we sit in silence.

A small tear escapes my eye. I will not admit it to Zeba, but it really breaks my heart to hear her talk like this. Is it too much to ask your children to understand the world through your eyes and experiences?

To accept truths that you have taken a lifetime to understand and comprehend? I feel tired. And deflated. May Allah show her the way. I have tried to teach her to the best of my knowledge, as a good parent should. *Now she is yours, Allah. Bas. Enough.*

We stop and get out of the car. I watch her as she strides away towards the holy spring. Despite my anger, I call after her to touch the water and to sprinkle some over her head, as is the custom. Then I watch from a distance as Zeba approaches the spring.

She bends down, but the moment her hands come in contact with the holy water, we are all blinded by a flash of lightning. I turn my head sharply to look at the sky. What was that? Just a random flash, out of nowhere?

When I look back at Zeba, I am aghast. I see her lying crumpled in a heap, face down in the water. Her body limp, as if the lightning has rendered her lifeless. I scream in panic and run towards her, stumbling, falling to my knees. Riyaz and the guards run past me.

Allah reham!

10

The Square Massacre Day, 1992

This day in 1992 may have been the beginning of the current, dark time in the history of Khudir, but if you really think about it, it all started on 8 April 1988, the day the Khan created oil in Khudir. That day, everyone in the country had rejoiced.

Allah hu Akbar! God is great! Oil in Khudir! How wonderful!

Every citizen of the kingdom thought it would make them rich and prosperous. But that oil money was cursed. It would never bring them any good. It was not real oil created by God over millennia in the underbelly of the Earth. It was oil created by *dark magic* by the evil Khan. It was oil created by greed. Pure insatiable avarice that was like an ever-hungry ogre, always craving for more.

Following that fateful day, in a short span of three years, things started changing rapidly. At first, people were happy. Happy to be rich. The oil created a lot of wealth for the Khan and other folks in Khudir. But then, as it often happens, the despot became greedier. He embarked on a journey to unlock the Cave of Magic to obtain the ancient magic Chaddor.

Naturally, people started to panic. Even the average citizen knew this was pushing it too far. The Chaddor had belonged to the family of the Akhoons, the First Tribe of Khudir, and was meant to do the bidding of the true heir of Akhoon. It was the symbol of Akhoon leadership and magical powers. The elders of Khudir had long realized that the Chaddor was very powerful. Too powerful for any one man to be allowed to possess it. With its power, a person could become unstoppable—do anything conceivable by the human mind, even perpetrate unthinkable horrors. So they agreed to lock it up in a cave and seal the entrance to it with magic. But the Khan, through sheer stubbornness and perseverance, had got his hands on the Chaddor.

He started wearing it everywhere he went. It made the people in Khudir very uncomfortable. Their soft murmurs grew stronger and bolder. *This is wrong. The ancestors do not want this.* And then whispers started in the palace corridors that the Khan had gone mad. From being called the Great Khan, he had now become the Mad Khan. He was going to attempt the forbidden. He wanted to wake up Yazoo. Yazoo—the darkest force known to man. A force that would open the doors of Hell on Earth. A force that would usher in the reign of Shaitan. But the Khan was willing to do this because the Mad Khan wanted to be King of the entire World.

He started combing through the population, picking up his targets for the Blood Ritual. The breaking point came when the people of Khudir finally protested and took to the streets. Enough was enough, they said. They could not allow this to keep happening. They appealed to the Khan to cease this madness, to stop invoking Yazoo. When he paid them no heed, at first, they organized marches and silent protests and candlelight vigils.

Then thousands of people set up camp in the Square.

They sat there for weeks. In the heat. All day. All night. Sang songs. Gave speeches. Wrote poetry. Shouted slogans. Banged vessels. Reporters from international news channels covered the protests and started showing them to the rest of the world.

'Local Khudirs Protesting the Khan's Evil Regime' read the headlines. International media christened it 'The Square Protest'. Of course, they had no idea what the locals were *actually* protesting. Because no Khudir local would ever talk about the magic, the Chaddor, the Blood Ritual, or Yazoo to a non-Khudir. Outsiders would not understand.

For the world, it was simply about human rights, democracy and civil rights. The stuff one sees on TV every few months. But the reality was different. Thousands of people were protesting an evil king's demonic activities and flagrant use of harmful magic. It was a *jihad* for the souls of the entire world.

Jihad—to fight or protest. In Islam, the greatest jihad is always with oneself. With the evil within you. After that comes the jihad with outside oppressors. But, even then, one must use all negotiations and diplomatic tactics first to settle matters without violence and fighting. So that's what our Khudir protestors did. They rallied—peacefully, patiently.

The protests dragged on for weeks, then months, and gradually the efforts of the people began to pay off, gather momentum. There was Ebrahim, who served as the singer and poet of the revolution, the voice of the people. He sang songs, recited poetry, and sometimes rapped all day long. He hoped that his words would keep people's morale high and pierce the heart of the Mad King and show him the truth.

'We will fight with our poetry.
Our words of love and of Peace.
Our words will be the bullets of this war.
Our songs will bring down this dictator.
We will Revolt.
Revolution Until Victory, my brothers and sisters.
Erase the darkness, my friends.'

Another protester, Sarah, worked in quieter ways. She was the earliest to wake in the morning and make tea for the entire makeshift camp. She would offer tea, medicines and cigarettes to everyone around the Square. They called her the Florence Nightingale of the protest. She had an aura about her that reassured everyone, helped them believe in the eventual success of the agitation.

Then there was the student Nagma, with her short-bleached hair and tattoos. She was studying at Isch School in Denmark before she left everything to return home to join the protestors. She was the one who sent videos and news to foreign correspondents.

These people and many others became important pillars of The Square Protest.

And while all this was happening, what did the Mad Khan do? Nothing.

On 8 April 1988, a photo of the Khan had appeared on the front page of the *New York Times* along with an image of the first oil-drilling machine. After that, the Khan had not spoken to the media or addressed his people. He never spoke on TV, gave no interviews, called no press conferences. Sure, you saw him moving around, wearing the Chaddor. But not a word from him on any matter found its way out from his lips.

Nothing. Radio silence.

But then, one day, after a particularly stinging piece was aired on CNN, that called him all sorts of names and mentioned threats of foreign sanctions, he decided he had had enough. That day, he walked out of the palace, fuming, and came to the Square. Alone. Wearing the Chaddor. And with little ceremony, he began to gun down the protestors.

Peaceful civilians were executed one by one. Shots of what looked like *electric currents* hit people as they fell dead. Daughters were killed in front of mothers, sons in front of fathers, parents before their children. Instantly. People yelled, screamed, ran about, cried for help. But the Khan was unstoppable. He thundered an order for everyone to stop.

Then, he summoned Ebrahim. The face of the revolution. Forcing Ebrahim to stand next to him, the Khan addressed the public. 'This man was your voice. This man's ugly music that you all are so intent on. See what I do to him. Don't be scared. I won't kill him. I will not make it that easy for him.' And in one stroke, he cut off Ebrahim's tongue.

Bleeding and in shock, Ebrahim fell to the ground. A collective gasp was heard, followed by absolute silence as the horror of this unspeakable act seeped through the Square. Only Ebrahim's painful grunts could be heard.

Everyone was shaken to their core. The same thought went through each mind: This Mad King is going to kill us all and create a mountain of our severed heads right here. All is lost.

'Stop! At once!' A booming voice had echoed through the silent Square. It had stopped the Mad King in his tracks. Umar, the Khan's brother, walked up to him. He was the only one who would dare to raise his voice at an enraged Khan.

Facing the Khan head on, Umar looked him in the eye. 'If you are planning to kill all these people here, you must kill me first.'

The Khan fumed and spluttered, but slowly he backed down. He couldn't kill his beloved brother. He turned and walked away. Leaving Umar alone in the Square with the bodies of the dead protestors and thousands of others weeping and mourning. Umar looked around to assess the situation. He knew what had to be done. 'Someone, call an ambulance,' he shouted. 'We have to take Ebrahim to the hospital!'

Umar was the Khan's only weakness. And that was not acceptable to the Khan. He couldn't just go against his heart and put his little brother to death. Instead, he threatened to kill Umar's children and his wife.

'I am the King, Umar!' he thundered. 'The King! If you choose to stand against me, whether in public or in private, I will sentence your entire family to death on account of treason.'

Umar lowered his head but stood his ground. 'Brother, my *imaan* will not allow me to stand by and watch such bloodshed.'

'Then leave! Otherwise, I swear I will have no option but to kill your entire family. And you too, if it comes to that. Trust me, I don't want to do that. So don't make me.'

Umar waited a long time before he finally spoke, his voice heavy with sadness. 'Fine. We will leave,' he said.

In return, the only promise Umar wanted was that the Khan would not harm any more protestors or their families. The Khan made a promise, but he was adamant that Umar leave as soon as possible, and that the Khan's authority was never again challenged, at home or abroad. 'Or the deal is off.'

Umar had no choice. Given the circumstances, this was the best bargain he could strike. Save his family, save the lives of the protestors—and leave his beloved land forever. A small price to pay.

In Khudir's history this day came to be known as the Square Massacre Day. No mention of Umar or the role he had played in saving thousands of lives was ever put on record. In the public domain, Umar was simply 'advised' to leave the country owing to political turmoil.

And so, three days later, after their final visit to Zsa Zsa and the other pilgrimage sites, Umar and Ayesha left Khudir with their boys.

And, of course, as we know, dear readers, with a new addition to their brood: Zeba.

11

Miracle #3

This is the moment when everything changed.

Flashes. Dreams. Hallucinations.
People. Places. Objects.

They appeared before her eyes.

Some images made sense. Some didn't. Some people, some faces she knew. Others seemed familiar, yet she had no memory of them.

She was awake, yet she wasn't. A strange kind of lucid dreaming. Like she had consumed Grade 3 government-approved health-council-regulated Amsterdam mushrooms. Magic mushrooms. Psilocybin that turns every experience into sheer delight upon ingestion.

Zeba felt as though she was being sucked into a deep tunnel. She was falling but her body was not reaching the ground. The tunnel was full of light. Vibrant colours. Glowing. Glistening surfaces. An unusual richness of textures.

When she landed, it was in a huge water body with a massive splash.

She was a baby. Lifeless, lying at the bottom of a pool of some kind. She was travelling back through time, seeing everything—a mix of things that made sense and things that didn't.

The face of an old bent woman, a midwife, a eunuch, a girl in childbirth, a black geometric cloak, an evil eye—the tunnel continued.

A sound.

An ancient hum.

Past and future all thrown together. As if someone had stepped inside her head and shuffled things around. Added to that, a few memories—some that seemed like hers, though she could not be sure; some that could not possibly be. Memories that belonged to others. To a young girl with a baby. To the towering figure beside her. To a little boy crying alone by the side of a mountain.

Zeba's thoughts were a confused mess of awe, wonder, anxiety, confusion, discomfort, helplessness.

Nothing made sense.

Time and space had warped. Zeba didn't know how long she was in this state of free fall, of this non-thinking awareness, this never-ending lucid dream. Was it an hour? Days? Weeks? Years? It felt like a few lifetimes.

Finally, she awoke. Drenched in sweat. Gasping for breath. Alive. Relieved.

Something had changed. She was unable to find the words to express her thoughts. She felt scared, and vulnerable, and yet somehow stronger than she'd ever been before. Her mind buzzed. She felt a sense of openness, of infinite possibility.

As her surroundings came into focus, she realized that she was in the palace. In her bed. How did she get here? What had happened? The ancient hum still rang in her ears. The dreams, the visions ... they overwhelmed Zeba.

Slowly, she pulled herself out of bed and made her way to the bathroom. She looked at herself in the mirror. *Fuck! I look like a mess.* She bent down to wash her face. *Wait a minute, is that an icicle stuck on the water faucet?* The glistening tap in the basin looked ordinary, except that the stream of water from the faucet had turned into ice.

Zeba blinked and looked around. *Err ... this still Khudir? Or have I been transported to an identical room in Antarctica with no heater?*

As soon as she touched the icicle, it transformed, leaping into a jet of scalding hot water. *Ouch!* Zeba jumped away, taken aback. She flinched, imagining the temperature of the water from which steam now rose. But her skin did not react to it.

What the fuck!

As she peered at the water faucet, now *behaving strangely and refusing to conform to Newtonian concepts,* she gasped out loud. The water seemed to have a life of its own. It was changing its form. After a few minutes of observing it, Zeba realized that the water's movements were reflecting the shifts in her own mood.

What the actual fuck!

Here, dear readers, I must fast-forward this part of the story because, if you ask me, it is the most boring bit. Because it deals with that completely overdone scenario: **How does a superhero respond to the sudden realization that she has superpowers?**

Disbelief, fear, excitement, experimentation ... Yaawwn. A staple in every story—a narrative you've read hundreds of times before. Yes, Zeba awakened with 'superpowers' and, yes, she was angry, confused, excited, fearful—all those things and more.

Suffice to say that suddenly Zeba found she could boil water or freeze it, depending on her mood and what she wanted the water to do. She could also control another person's body temperature (since the human body is 70 per cent water) and shoot sharp streams of water from her wrists when excited or attacked. Or both. And, yes, she performed numerous experiments driven by despair and disbelief.

As she explored her newfound powers, she shot darts of water all across the room causing considerable damage to the rather gorgeous and pristine quarters. She also managed to give her poor driver, Riyaz, a fever, froze (and thawed) the palace puppy Shera, water-blasted chairs and several objects around her. In fact, the only good that came out of these experiments was that some indoor plants got watered a few additional times.

Anyway, you get the idea.

As she explored her powers, she realized she was not happy. It gave her no pleasure to be a bigger freak than she had grown used to being.

Weirdo. Weirdo. Weirdo.

The word became a chant in her head. A familiar word, a favourite of her middle-school classmates who had bullied her. She knew she had to seek help. And the only person she could turn to was her mother.

Zeba silently endured the many well-meaning yet overbearing ministrations of her mother who was in Mommy Will Fix It mode. Ayesha chanted verses from the Quran and tied an amulet to Zeba's arm, believing that perhaps this was some kind of evil dark magic or *nazar* that must be tackled.

Allah Huma Inni ... blah blah blah ...

All through it, singular thought sat heavy on Zeba's mind: *This day is not a good one.*

Zeba was right. Let's just say that, on an average, the day most superheroes discover their superpowers is not their best. Nor their brightest. Nor the most glory-filled.

She muttered what all those in this situation would say to themselves at this point.

FUCK THIS (SUPERHERO) SHIT.

12

A Royal Wedding

A gold-sequinned dress with tassels. (Okay, less a dress and more an ornate swimsuit, but not good for *actual* swimming. Only posing. Strutting. Dancing.)

Knee-high gold boots.

Long, cascading curly hair.

Six stage blowers angled to blow the hair back just perfectly.

Thighs that evoked lust and dreams of earth-shattering orgasms among all genders.

And a voice to match.

Poised. Polished. Fierce.

'We're smart enough to make these millions.
Smart enough to bear these children,
Then get back to business.'

'I ... I likeeee that song,' a slightly inebriated Zeba said at the top of her voice, as she watched Queen Bey perform on a newly constructed stage in the middle of the palace grounds. Thankfully, no one heard her because of the thundering music and the sea of women going wild around her.

It was Sangeet Night and the house was on fire. The state-of-the-art stage had been erected just for this event with the gorgeous dome of the main palace building serving as its background. The star of the night closed her performance with a levitation act, followed by a display of fireworks the likes of which had never been seen before.

The Akhoon palace grounds had been decked up in red and gold. Apart from the State guests, the ladies of the harem were in attendance, the Sultan's wives and concubines—all forty-one of them—the only women in hijabs, the hidden stars of the show whose faces were not for plebians to behold. Usually, they sat in a special enclosure, but today the rules were a bit relaxed, and they were socializing with guests. Palace rumour had it that one of the wives had gifted Beyonce a gold abaya. Not gold-like or golden in colour, but *gold*—an abaya made from 24 karat gold threads.

It was an odd sight. Two vastly different worlds colliding, or shall we say coexisting, at this raging private concert in a land far, far away from Western civilization. A blend of partygoers in smart, tailored suits and in local traditional attire, women in a mix of mini-skirts and gorgeously embellished outfits wearing impossible Jimmy Choos and elegant hijab-covered oddities. Almost surreal.

'Harrrrrem,' said Zeba, rolling the word around in her mouth like a delicious piece of ice on a hot summer night. 'Doesn't that mean forbidden?' she asked, turning to her mother, who had been her annoying prayer-muttering shadow since her embarrassing life-altering Zsa Zsa incident.

'Classic mistake,' she heard a booming voice say from behind her.

Zeba turned around and found herself face to face with a rather intimidating, opaque royal blue hijab. She could barely see the piercing eyes behind the veil.

'Classic *gora* mistake,' said the hijab with the voice.

Gora. White. Western.

Zeba took in the two female guards flanking this figure before her and gulped. The royal blue hijab and the extra female security could mean only one thing. This was the Khan's first wife.

'Salaam, Sultana. A ... a pleasure to meet you,' she finally blurted out.

The Khan's first wife ignored the customary greeting and continued, 'You are mixing up the words "haraam" and "harem". "Haraam" means forbidden. The word you said is "harem", which comes from the Arabic word "haram", meaning a private or sacred place.'

Zeba bent forward, bowing awkwardly. Very few occurrences threw the usually smug Zeba, and this was one of them. She hadn't anticipated meeting any of the veiled creatures, let alone being addressed by one of them. Even though they were 'related', so to speak, and, well, it was a family wedding, Zeba had not met any of the ladies of the harem during any of the insufferable meals they had had with the Great Khan. The lack of interaction had seemed suspiciously engineered to Zeba, but now here she was, stuttering before one of them.

'But then ...' said Zeba, momentarily regaining her cockiness, '... not much is forbidden here in Khudir, I guess.' She gestured at the debauchery unfolding around them. As if on cue, a waiter passed by them bearing questionable substances on a silver tray.

'Well,' the voice drawled. 'You are right. But we *all* ...'—a sufficiently lengthy pause followed—'... choose *convenience* in that way, do we not? Customizing life and rules, and making it all up as we chug along?'

Fuck, wow! This woman has a way of silencing you.

The Sultana continued. 'Yes. We *all* follow what is *convenient,* what makes sense to us and what we want to project to the outside world. Our Great Khan is no different. He likes some rules, and he likes to break the ones that don't serve him. You, Zeba, also don't like rules *very* much, do you?'

Zeba thought she heard a hint of a smile in the voice.

I am sure you will come visit us soon in the Harem Quarters. We make for good conversation, us *harem* women.' Then she strode away without waiting for a response.

Only after the classy figure disappeared into the crowd did Zeba find her swag again. 'Wow, must have a beer with that one. She'll have some juicy *dirty* stories about the Khan,' she remarked with a chuckle.

'Nah! He probably just rolls over and snores in bed,' she heard Ayesha say in a deadpan voice.

Zeba opened her eyes wide. 'Ammi! You be careful. I'm afraid you might be catching a sense of humour!'

13

The Afterparty

The next morning, Instagram stories, the news headlines of every newspaper and X feeds would proclaim 'US Singer Beyonce performs as part of the lavish festivities at the extravagant wedding of Khudir's Crown Prince', etc., etc., etc. But on this night, the ladies in Khudir were having a night to remember.

'If you like it, then you should'a put a ring on it
If you like it, then you should'a put a ring on it
Don't be mad once you see that he want it ...'

This stellar, no-expenses-spared performance was at the bride's special request. But perhaps we must thank the stars that no one had informed or would inform Queen Bey that her private concert for the Crown Prince's future wife and the ladies of Khudir was *not* the most important event to take place that night. Fate had other plans—and was leading Zeba away from all this revelry, towards something else.

Drunk on too much wine, our story's protagonist walked away from the noise and celebration towards the quietest corner of the palace garden. She had managed to ply her mother with a few glasses, too, and escape her watchful eye.

Alone, finally.

She allowed herself to feel the confusion and sadness she had been fighting since arriving in Khudir and being zapped by Zsa Zsa. The alcohol eased her defences. Still, it was not a good combination for a lost superhero with untamed strong powers. She looked at the Graeco-Roman-architecture-inspired water fountain and decided to test out her newfound abilities.

Stop water. Flow water. Stop ... Freeze. Thaw. Boil.

That's a better rhythm, she slurred in her head.

Stop. Freeze. Thaw. Boil.

That's good practice. And I'm a confirmed weirdo.

Far away from the newly constructed crowded performance hall where everyone was swaying to 'Drunk in Love', Zeba was free to try out her powers without being seen. So she carried on.

Until suddenly—noises.

Zeba stopped. She thought she heard two voices. Loud, argumentative.

The younger son of the Khan, Sayed, and his trusted aide.

Sayed sounded sad and angry.

Same pinch, cousin.

'This is such a waste,' Sayed was saying, sounding shrill and frustrated. 'Have they not seen the plight of the poor people of the kingdom?'

Oops. I think Sayed may have had a few extra goblets of wine, thought Zeba as she turned to sneak away without being noticed.

'No one listens to me,' Sayed continued. 'They think I am a fool. A child. A pussy. That is what Father ... No, that's what the Khan says. The Khan says do this, do that ... he sees *nothing*. He *feels* nothing. He is not a man. He is a monster. I have seen him doing bad things. He is not human. He is ...'

The aide hushed Sayed. This was dangerous talk, even in private. If anyone heard them, they'd both hang for treason.

But Sayed was in no mood to stop. 'No, my father is evil! I am telling you. My brother is evil. And I have their blood. So I must be evil too, right? But I am not. I try to ... I am a good man ... Am I not?'

'Yes, Your Highness, you are a good man,' said the aide. 'You are just tired. I must take you to your room.'

Zeba knew better than to get involved in palace politics. *Not my monkey, not my circus.* She slowly started to tiptoe back to her quarters. But, as luck would have it, halfway through her escape, just as she started to pick up speed—*Wham!* She collided into someone.

The Bollywood hottie. RK.

Damn, he's hot.

He smiled. She smiled. Both swayed in merry drunkenness.

In a movie, they'd have talked and looked at the stars. Held hands, or something romantic like that. But this was not a movie.

'Hey,' said RK.

'Hi.'

'This is your date for the night? Brother Sayed? I know you're allowed to date and marry first cousins, but ... didn't think he was your type.'

Zeba smiled, enjoying the flirting, but walked away, saying, 'Rubbish!'

'Hey, you're abandoning me?'

'Looks like it, doesn't it?'

Silence, and a long moment of gazing into each other's eyes.

Finally, RK said, 'Come to my room.'

'Nope. You come to mine.'

'Okay. I will follow you, madam.'

'Come, but we will only talk. I can make you chamomile tea, and ... Bring a lighter.'

RK followed, knowing full well that she was only being coy.

As soon as they were indoors, safely in the confines of Zeba's room ... Well, you know what happened next, reader. What always does.

Brevity is the name of the lusty game. It took little time for passionate kissing to escalate into the two eagerly ripping off each other's clothes in perfect madness and haste.

Ah! Drunk in Lust.

What a wonderful end to the night.

Or was it?

The thing about real life is that the stories never end where one expects them to ...

Post-coitus RK was happily snuggling up to sleep. Deep, restful, relieved sleep. But Zeba knew better than to let Mr Hot Bollywood Hookup spend the night. Come dawn and the palace would be crawling with people, buzzing with activity. She shook him hard and pulled him to his feet.

'You have to go. I'm not being rude, but you *cannot* be seen in my room, or bed, or leaving my room. So ... go go go.'

'I get it ... but damn you're harsh!'

'Sorry, just being practical ... Go go go.'

'Okay fine. Later? Again?'

'Done.'

'Okay bye.'

RK was almost halfway out the door when he turned back and flashed her his million-dollar movie-star smile. 'I like you. You're cool.'

Zeba groaned and threw a pillow at him. 'Tell me in the morning!'

He giggled and left on tiptoe.

As much as we like RK and think he is hot, and as much Zeba enjoyed these twenty minutes of hot sex, I regret to inform you that RK no longer plays an important role in our story after this episode. His primary job was to let our leading lady blow off some steam. This superhero stuff is stressful, after all. (And it's about to get even more so ...)

Zeba shut her door and smiled. *What a cute idiot. Who giggles like that? Man, I would like to see him again.*

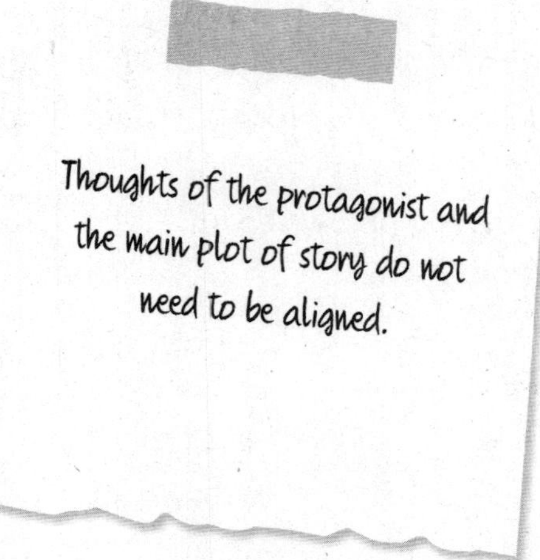

She walked back towards her bed, smiling, singing, humming.

As she rested her head on the pillow, without warning, a hand came out of nowhere and covered her mouth. Her eyes widened in horror, as she struggled against the force. The last thing she remembered before passing out were the terrifying red eyes of the presence behind a mask.

14

An Abduction

My head is exploding.

Have they hit me? I don't think so. But the pain inside my head is excruciating ... What is happening? All I can see is darkness because my eyes have been blindfolded.

What did the masked man cover my face with? Some kind of sedative? I must try to stay awake. Focus, Zeba. DO NOT PASS OUT...

So hazy, everything around me ... How long have I been out? It feels like hours, or days even. Is that ... two men, or three? Where are they taking me? I see a bridge, a forest ... or perhaps just a few trees ... followed by the desert. My eyes feel so heavy, but I must keep awake.

Why can't I hear anything? Just the hooves of the horses galloping ... Or is that a jeep? Maybe a truck?

How far are we from the palace? Did anyone see me being taken away? How did the man enter my room ... in spite of all the security around us?

Feel. So. Drugged.

My senses are numb. I want to fight back. Scream. Shout out curses. Free my wrists, open my blindfold. But I am unable to. I try to use my new powers, but I can't focus.

Every time I come to, I make another attempt. Perhaps I can summon enough anger or courage this time ... muster the strength and perform one of my newfound water tricks. What was it? Freeze, Boil ...

ARGHHHHH!

I'm unable to move a muscle. I feel weak, helpless. I open my lips to plead. Scream for help. But not a sound emerges, no words come out. My mind fills with unpleasant thoughts. I wonder what is in store for me. Are they going to kill me, maim me, rape me?

Who are these people? Jihadis? Locals rebels? Warring tribes? Definitely someone sick of the royal family and the injustices of the Great Khan. Am I their first hapless victim, the first abductee? Why did they choose me from among all those people at the party?

Well, an American hostage in an Islamic dictatorship ... surely that means some leverage? My life must be worth *something*. But why pick *me*? It could've been any of the others ... my brothers, my parents, the ladies from the harem, Sayed ... RK?

Oh no! Did somebody see me gulp down wine and have sex with a man I'm not married to? Is it the morality police of this land? Anything seems plausible in this mad world. I am the outsider. Worse, I am the insider who looks like them but has given up on their customs, religion, morals and way of life.

The bad person. The immoral girl. The threat.

Maybe they want to hang me ... Punish me as a cautionary tale for other 'wayward' women who refuse to obey orders?

All those YouTube videos showing women being lynched because they have been adulterous or had pre-marital sex. Fuck fuck fuck! I NEED TO GET OUT OF HERE NOW.

I try to scream, beg, plead, but can only manage a whimper.

And what is this now? We've stopped. I can hear footsteps. Someone pulls me out, throws me on the ground, removes my blindfold.

I let my eyes adjust to being able to see and take in my surroundings. A cave of some sort. Sand all over the ground, but the floor is covered in rugs. I am too sacred to look up. To look my captor in the eye. Afraid to see his face because then I will definitely not be allowed to live.

My heart is racing and every nerve in my body tells me to get up and run, I start begging, blabbering. 'I am just here to attend a wedding. Please ... I don't know anything. Please let me go. I am a good person. A good girl. Not *kafir*.'

Then I stop. This is the end, I tell myself. I will never go home again. Never see Abba–Amma, my brothers, Doobie ... ever again. This is it.

'Look at me,' a voice echoes. It doesn't belong to anyone I know, yet it sounds strangely familiar.

I raise my head, scared. Finally, I see my captor without a mask.

An imposing figure looks at me with what seems like a stern expression.

'Hello, Zeba, my child. I have been waiting for you. We have so much to talk about ...'

15

Army of the Pure

Old age is a terrible teacher. Yet, to be honest, God has been kind to me.

Alhamdulillah.

I think I am stronger, more agile in my fifties than I was in my twenties. The hard work, the horse riding, and the morning runs have served me well. After my namaz, I start my day with an hour of callisthenics and running, followed by stretching.

But I now need a weekly massage, else my muscles start knotting up and that causes a lot of pain. To be honest, there are days when the hard callused hands of my aide take me back to the days spent at the hammam in the palace. Those stolen days. Almost from another time. It is true: Luxury can make your soul a slave forever. Even in memory. One must strive very hard not to let such thoughts permeate one's mind. For such thoughts alone are the first step towards corruption.

Sigh.

Maybe I am just being nostalgic about the days gone by. Unabashed nostalgia is one of the few luxuries I can still afford. I have a huge responsibility on my shoulders now. Entrusted to me by God Almighty. To lead his army. The last Army of the Pure.

However, this army is not made of soldiers; it is an army of spies. The only people left in this kingdom who are following God's word in the way it should be. Those who are resisting Shaitan. The evil force. Those who are fighting every day against oppressors, terror-mongers, tyrants, dictators and despotic regimes like the Taliban, Al-Qaeda, ISIS, the Mad Khan and all manner of organizations and individuals who are damaging the image of the Muslim faith all over the world.

'Islam' means submission to the will of God. Submission and total devotion. The word itself comes from 'sal'm', meaning 'peace'. Islam embodies peace and tolerance. Complete submission to creating a world that stands for empathy and love, by the will of God Almighty.

When the good word of Islam spread all over the globe, like flavour from a tea bag seeps into a hot cup of water, it transformed the whole world. Slaves were freed. Women were given rights. Education was made accessible to all. But evil men have conniving ways to corrupt even the word of the Almighty. Evil men take everything good and beautiful and manipulate it to suit their purpose. Evil men see only hate in the world and can trade in hate alone. Their parochial hearts are bereft of love and empathy. They do not see the bounty of our Allah; they see only sin and *zinah*. Their minds are trained by darkness to intensify darkness. Their hearts eternally feed on sorrow, grief and trauma.

Darkness is an addiction.

There is a reason our Allah forbade us from consuming anything that could make addicts out of us, makes us its slaves. Addiction creates obsession and an unhealthy dependence, often making men and women behave unlike themselves. They lose the ability to distinguish between good and bad. They lose focus and their core humanity. They lose themselves. Every act born of addiction is, for us believers, a sin.

And darkness is the biggest addiction known to humanity, the most dangerous addiction of them all.

Idle humans dwell on dark thoughts. Their minds are trained to see the world as ugly. They go so far as to hate even their own bodies.

God Almighty asked us to cover our bodies to shade them from darkness and the evil eyes of other men. He was telling us how to protect and shield our bodies from the foulness around us. But see how sly men can be. They cunningly interpreted his word and made it seem that God had commanded us to cover our bodies because they need to be hidden from sight. They altered it to imprisonment. Connected it to ugliness. Whereas it was always about decency, attitude and modest behaviour. It was always about conducting yourself in a dignified manner.

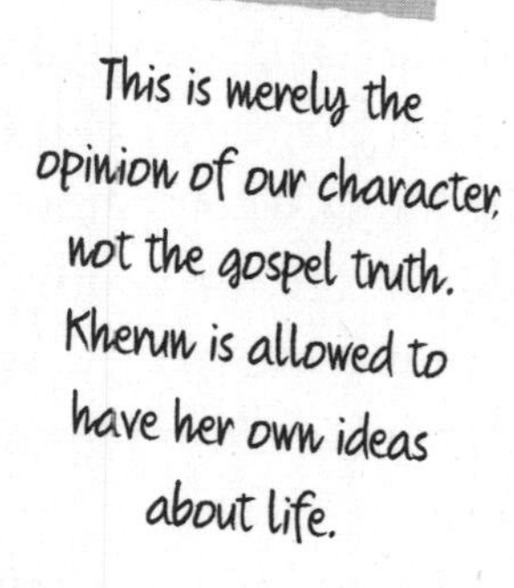

Addicts of darkness are hard to save. Their souls are so dark that sometimes even the Light of Allah and the Absolute Truth cannot touch them.

Evil. Darkness. Shaitan.

Darkness and Shaitan exist in everyone and everything. First, one must try to change that with empathy.

Taubah. Forgiveness. Mercy.

Only if that does not work should one turn to the last resort, which is to pick up arms.

But people are aching to kill, shoot, fight without first using their hearts to heal and change the world. Evil men in positions of power are the biggest impediment towards God's work. In my long life I have seen many evil men up close. Bad men who hired me to spy on others, pass on messages, to handle all their shady business. I was born in poverty, so for me my hunger, or rather my fear of going hungry, was motivation enough to bow my head and do the bidding of these men.

Many a day I have cried till my eyes were swollen, yet I have served them all. Businessmen, tribal chiefs, even some foreign politicians. Been forced to do corrupt deeds for them. But no master I served was as evil as the Mad Khan. He is so consumed by darkness that there is no Redemption for him whether in this world or the next. He has killed and maimed without mercy, raped and burned without remorse. He is a glutton and, worst of all, he thinks of himself as, *nau-zu-billah*, an equal to GOD.

But one day, I knew I had had enough. I could do it no more. It was the day I killed you.

The Mad Khan has to be stopped before it is too late for all of us. He has to be brought down. And if I have to give my life to make sure it is done, I will. With a smile on my face. I will be God's mercenary. My Allah's foot soldier. If necessary, I will die trying to stop this man from bringing injustice and pain upon God's Holy Land.

All these years, I have been waiting. Working in the shadows. Living at the edge of cities. Never in one place. Helping many flee this land. Smuggling people out. Stopping the king's soldiers from plundering villages and raping women. I have always known how unsafe it is to do what I do. The slightest misstep and a sword or spear will be rammed through my heart. But I have to do it. I am the one God has chosen.

Zeba, my child, I know this is too much to take in. I know what I have told you is hard to fathom. But it is all true.

I was the one who took you to the holy Zsa Zsa to drown you. I was whom your dying mother begged to perform that unholy task. When I first laid eyes on you, a crying, wailing infant, covered in blood and embryonic fluid, I thought you were a cursed child. Better dead than alive. I did not imagine you would survive the unspeakable act I committed.

But you changed me, my child. As I left you to die alone that day, a mere, helpless baby, my tears would not stop flowing. My heart was shattered. After your mother's quick and sad burial, I packed a few belongings and left that cursed palace. I walked for hours and hours. My sin weighed so heavily on me that I thought I would start rotting. I walked for days without food, without water. I lost all sense of time.

Then, one day, I do not know how or after how long, I found myself in a cave. It was dark and I was alone. I had pulled out my hair. My skin was dry and scaly. My lips parched, feet covered in blisters and calluses. I lay on the ground with a hard rock as a pillow. I wanted to die. I prayed to Allah to end my wicked life, in which I had known only shame.

First, as a eunuch, I was ridiculed. Then I brought shame upon myself. I worked as a pimp and spy for the worst kind of man. I did every kind of bad deed for him in exchange for bread and a roof over my head. I brought him your beautiful mother, a poor goatherd's daughter. When the Khan laid eyes on her at a function he attended in her school, she was barely thirteen. When he returned, he could hardly contain himself. He told me he wanted her picked up, cleaned and perfumed, and presented to him. I did it. I groomed your mother for him. It is a shame I shall carry with me always.

I held your sobbing mother in my arms after that man violated her for the first time. I allowed it to happen. Oh, I will never forgive myself. All the while, I kept telling myself that I *had* to do it. That I had no choice. That if I did not do it someone else would and the King would just throw me out on the road. Where would I go? What would I do? Who am I, after all? Just a *hijra*. A mere eunuch. A nobody.

But somewhere in my heart, I knew it was not true. I had a choice. I always had a choice. I did not have to be such a lowlife.

The evening I left you for dead, I apologized to my Allah for every sin I had committed. With your innocent baby face floating before my eyes, I recited the verses from the Quran my mother had taught me. Whatever I could remember, I kept saying again and again. I was looking for forgiveness in those holy verses. Asking for forgiveness in the afterlife.

'Forgive me lord in my *akhirat*. Forgive me.'

I rubbed my nose on the hard rock.

Taubah taubah taubah.

'Forgive me in my final hours on this earth.'

I knew I was better off dead than alive.

But Allah did not take my life. Instead, he chose to give me a vision.

That night, in my dreams, I saw you. You were the baby I had left in the cold spring water. It was undoubtfully you, but you were different.

You seemed in my dream a few days older, perhaps. You were happy and well fed, and in a strange land. You had a diaper on and a shawl with a 'Z' embroidered on it.

I woke up with a start.

How is this possible, I asked myself. I wondered if I was going mad. Was my mind playing hallucinatory tricks? I had left that poor child to die. Could God have saved her? Was it possible?

I managed to slowly get on my knees, my body broken but my heart singing. Could my Allah have saved this innocent life and saved me from the ultimate sin? I stayed in the cave for a few days and every night I dreamt of you, my Zeba. Every night I saw you. Since that first night, my Allah has shown me your face in my dreams nightly.

He has shown me all the signs. I have watched you grow up, one day at a time, from hundreds of miles away. I watched you take your first step, scrape your knee, sulk over a broken heart. I have witnessed your rage and your excitement. Your confusion. Your hurt and your pain. I know it sounds unbelievable, my child. But it is all true. It is a miracle. *You* are a miracle.

I knew through my visions that someday you would come back. And I knew I had to wait for you. I knew that God had in his infinite wisdom had found a purpose for your innocent life. And I knew I had a role to play in God's plans. He wants me to do something to stop this darkness from spreading.

Since that day, I have been waiting. I have gathered this small army of broken souls and lost people. Waiting to be saved in some way. We have all been waiting for you to return. Waiting for our saviour.

All these people have lost someone, some have lost their homes, others lost an eye, their tongue or a limb. But none of them ever lost hope. Hope of being freed from this living hell. Hope of being citizens of a free nation. Hope for a better life. Every day, we have rescued someone or other from the wrath of this madman. This Army of the Pure works undercover all over the kingdom, helping those in the most need, providing them safe houses and shelters when they are hunted by the Khan. Sometimes we loot the royal food reserves and distribute rice and other staples to the hungry. We secretly pillage medical supplies for the unwell and diseased. We, the Army of the Pure, cannot openly fight the King but we help the poor Khudirs with the basics—food, water, medicines, life—which their King has failed to do for them.

This is how we have kept the rebellion going. They know about my visions and that powerful Akhoon blood flows in your veins. My visions and all their interpretations suggested only one thing: You were meant to come to us and put an end to the hateful regime of the Khan. And so, while we have fought every day in whatever way we can, we have tracked my dreams and waited for you to arrive.

A few days ago, in my dream, you were standing by the water fountain in the palace, and you called out my name. It was impossible. You, at the Royal Palace? And how would you know my name? But anything is possible in the realm of dreams. And one thing was certain—the time had come for us to meet.

I know I am a stranger to you. And I know how confusing this must be for you. Have patience, my child. God Almighty shall guide us. I simply know that I am supposed to protect you till the end of my days. I am to be your shield and guard. I am to hold your hand as you make your way through darkness.

I have told you everything I know ... The truth about the evil King and his atrocities, and you already know about the fabled Chaddor. It is time I told you the truth about your mother.

That is why, today, I wanted to bring you back to the same cave where God gave me my first vision of you ... To tell you this story. *Our story.*

Come now. Our soldiers are patiently waiting outside in anticipation. They have been waiting forever for this day. To see you. To see the girl whom Allah saved, upon whom Zsa Zsa bestowed another life. The girl who is the answer, for this fight to end in our favour, for all the ugliness in the world to stop.

Come, just a few steps more ...

Ah, don't turn away from me, little Zeba. Don't walk away ... Are you crying, my child? My mistake, of course, you can't cry, my Zeba. I can see how burdened you are by these revelations from your past. But look at how our soldiers regard you, how they strain to catch a glimpse of the chosen one. I know all this is sudden and confusing. You sit so far away with your back to us, your eyes searching the clear night sky for stars twinkling back at you. Your mind may be too clouded to hear what the stars want to tell you, but you must listen.

When I walk up to you and touch your shoulder, I hear you say softly, 'I want to know more about my past, my mother. I want to understand why this happened to her, to me. Where do we begin?'

Well, yes, my child. The best place to start is always from the beginning. Let me take you to see your mother. Her grave is not very far from here ...

I want to say more. Something right, something to give you strength. Some hope. But ... O Allah! What is that commotion? And the piercing screams that tear through the air?

Ahhhhh ... This is what I was afraid would happen.

THE KHAN'S SOLDIERS ARE HERE!

16

The First Showdown

Total chaos has ensued. The Army of the Pure is surrounded by the Great Khan's guards.

I sit with my back towards Kherun, further away from the other soldiers, on a small hillock. Once we emerged from the cave, I walked away, trying to keep calm, to catch a breath of fresh air and to borrow and smoke a cigarette. I understood the emotion with which Kherun had brought me to the cave, to show me where she had her first vision that connected me to her. But honestly that cave gave me the creeps. And after what she's told me about my mother, I can't bear the stale air and the dampness.

When the screams of 'The Khan's soldiers are here!' pierce the night, I turn, petrified, towards Kherun. My first instinct is to duck behind some rocks for cover. But Kherun stands tall, towering, unflinching.

Hiding in panic behind the boulders, I hear Bassam's voice booming out commands and threats. 'You have abducted my cousin,' he says. 'A royal! It is forbidden to spill royal blood on our Great Land. Surrender her or face our wrath. In the name of the King, the Great Khan, I command you!'

From my vantage point I can see Bassam standing with only a few soldiers. He looks like he is waiting for backup and would rather Kherun surrenders peacefully.

Then I hear Kherun scream back, 'Over our dead bodies, Bassam! Following us here was a mistake. Tonight's encounter may just cost you your wedding.'

Shit, this is going down real bad real fast. My head is spinning, I can hear my heart racing in my ears. Every instinct tells me this isn't going to end well. And what is with these guns and weapons? I'm tempted to yell out to Bassam, my cousin ... no, my *brother!* Can we just cut the drama and have an adult conversation, please? Let's be civilized about this and not indulge in all this melodrama. In fact, call the Great Khan too ...

Wait a minute. Do I have to call him *dad* now? I mean, does he even know? Damn, this is going to be a very tough conversation, and I need Kherun to be alive to tell him this.

Heck, I don't even have proof that anything Kherun has said is true. It does sound too outrageous, too cuckoo, too wild ... *to be made up*. My father abducted and forcefully married my teenage mother? I'm not sure how I'm supposed to feel about that. Why did my real father have to be such an asshole? How can I be happy about meeting (correction, *being re-acquainted with*) the man who is the reason for my mother's death? And how many times am I allowed to call him an asshole?

Asshole.

Asshole.

Asshole.

More screams and mayhem ... This isn't good. Nope. This isn't the fun night I had anticipated. I should be in bed, dreaming of Mr Bollywood, touching myself tenderly and planning our next coitus. How did I even get here?

Stop! Calm your internal chatter, woman. Time to shut down this external soon-to-erupt war.

From behind the shelter of the rocks, I summon some courage to assess the stand-off and spot Kherun, who has made her way down from the safe hillock, towards a group of the AOTP—yes, yes, Army of the Pure—soldiers in some sort of an attack formation.

I feel suddenly annoyed with her. Why did she have to drag me into this? This isn't my fight. I shouldn't be here. My heart is filled with fury. Yet now, looking at the AOTP organize themselves so promptly, I'm beginning to get why Kherun is so unafraid, and marvel at how valiantly she leads her small group. Its inspiring to see so much courage, nobility and passion for justice and the greater good. But I'm still quite certain I'd like to witness it from a safer spot and not as the epicentre of a hostage drama.

Kherun stands facing the enemy, a relic from an era gone by. Long hennaed hair flying in the wind, eyes rimmed with kohl, tall and majestic. There is a noble aura about her. She and her Army of the Pure seem ready to end their lives at this very instant for their cause.

Well, let's be honest. This isn't much of an *army*. More a ragtag group of really passionate folks armed with country-made guns and swords, even axes and brooms. Anything they can defend themselves with. Looking at their immaculate valour, something shifts in me.

What did these guys believe in?

The greater good and peace.

Who are they?

Good Muslims.

What are they fighting for?

Peace and prosperity.

What are they fighting against?

Bloodshed and killing in the name of Allah.

Surely there is more nobility in this group than I have ever seen in my silly, hollow life. I realize quite suddenly that there is a certain beauty in being madly passionate about something. It makes you strong and fragile at the same time. Resilient yet breakable.

I also see what these people are up against. Not to be harsh, but this is a losing game. They are never going to win, which is why perhaps they have never fought the Khan's soldiers face to face. Always from the shadows, in some form of guerrilla warfare. Looting food godowns and water reserves, helping kidnapped reporters and young women escape from captivity. Sure, Bassam has all of fifteen soldiers with him right now. But there is no doubt that the whole damn army is on its way to annihilate this ragtag group of the AOTP.

I don't feel good about this fight. Am I responsible in some way for what's about to happen? I must be—if all that Kherun has told me is true. About my birth and my birth parents ... I have so many questions ... especially about my mother ...

Mom. Ammi. M ... M ... Miriam. And ... this tyrant King.

The Khan is my dad. The Khan is my dad. The Khan is my dad.

Fuck. So that makes me a princess of Khudir? One of the women of the harem?

Fuck fuck fuck!

My head starts spinning again. I want to puke. Damn, that concert-party seems so far away now. I would do anything to go back to just a few hours ago. And stay there.

'Surrender!' screams Bassam, his voice cutting through the thick night air of Khudir. Seriously? That delivery would make a dog's ears bleed. Bassam sure loves the sound of his own voice.

But Kherun doesn't get a chance to respond. Nor do I.

Bang!

The first bullet of the night pierces through the air and lodges itself straight in the heart of a foot soldier of Army of the Pure.

'Nagma, noooo!' Kherun's cry is just as loud as the sound of the bullet, just as horrifying.

It seems one of the King's guards had quietly sneaked off and found a vantage point from where he had a clean shot at Kherun. He knew if he took out Khudir's Public Enemy #1 he would be well rewarded. And taking out the commander-in-chief of the enemy side would instantly tilt the conflict in Bassam's favour. So he aimed for Kherun's heart and fired. Except, Nagma threw herself in front of Kherun just in time to save her from the rogue bullet.

Kherun is swiftly by Nagma's side, whose left shoulder looks pretty messed up. I'm frozen to the spot; this is entirely too much for me to process.

Then Nagma falls down. Dead.

Okay, this is that nice lady everyone likes in the group. The kind lady with the tattoos. *Damn!* Things are about to spiral out of control, aren't they?

'Attack!' Kherun yells, her eyes bloodshot.

FUCK!

Mayhem.

Run, Zeba, run. Hide your ass away.

Bullets fly past me as I scramble for cover behind the rocks. My foot slides and I skid down the side of the hillock. Fuck no. I have to get out of here. Damn. I'm out in the open now ... one stray bullet is all it'll take!

There are some jeeps and a huge armoured truck parked at the bottom of the incline. Perfect to hide behind. I half run half crawl in the general direction of the vehicles. A bullet flies too close to my right ear, and I instinctively let out a scream.

Finally, I reach the armoured truck, running past the AOTP soldiers who are firing their weapons at the enemy. They give me dirty looks. I know what they are thinking. 'Seriously? *This* is the woman we went to all this trouble for? *She's* supposed to fight for *us*!'

I see the repulsion in their eyes. Anger. Hurt. Disappointment. Abandonment. But I'm too scared to feel any shame. Every fibre of my being is telling me to just get out of there. So I keep running. Farther and farther, towards the cave. But it's too far and I need to change course. I make a dash for the armoured truck. Maybe I can hide in the back. Wait for it all to get over.

I reach the truck and am about to climb in, when two royal soldiers jump me. They grab me by the arms. We wrestle. Well, *I* wrestle. They seem to have a pretty stable grip on me.

I don't want to go with these guys. I still have questions about my past, my birth mother. I need to know what the fuck happened.

I struggle but these soldiers don't budge. Damn their red meat diets and warrior workouts. And then, one of them hits me on the head with the butt of his gun.

That was uncalled for.

NOOOOOOOOOOOOOOOOOOOOOOOOOOOOOOO!

I'm yelling only partly in pain. The rest is seething anger. How dare they!

But the scream does something unexpected. Jets of water shoot out from my hands, hitting the soldiers like a power hose. The two go flying and land on one of the parked jeeps with loud THUDs and slide to the ground, limp.

I look down at my hands, stunned. What did I just do?

Should have done this sooner, I realize, but how was I to know that under duress my senses would conjure up this kind of spontaneous force? I thought it all depended on my moods!

I see another guard making his way towards me. Instinctively, I raise my right hand to protect myself. Again, an unexpected jet of water shoots out. This one tosses the guard even farther away.

Woah!

These water jets I'm shooting out can throw objects over long distances without dissipating. Look at the guard and the vehicle that were in my way. Both flung back by at least 100 metres.

By now, everyone has stopped in their tracks and is looking at me. They can't believe their eyes. My weirdo-meter has officially hit 'broken'.

Everyone looks at me, petrified. I spot Kherun a short distance from me. She was fighting hand to hand with a soldier, who now stands transfixed in a defensive posture. She has a strange smile on her lips.

Bassam is the first to regain his composure. He shouts at his guards to start firing again. 'Kill them all!' he thunders.

But it is my turn. 'Stop!' I yell.

By now, my body and mind are in sync. I instinctively know what to do. I raise my hands. All the soldiers stop in mid-motion, their boots stuck to the ground, frozen to their spots. The guns in their hands are instantly jammed with ice. Bassam's men drop their frozen guns to the ground where they shatter into a million little icicles. The remaining royal guards are in shock. I'm sure no one has ever witnessed anything like this. Some of them start shivering and fall to their knees, asking for mercy.

Jaadu. Magic. Kala jaadu. Dark magic. They whisper among themselves.

Bassam looks at me, shooting daggers. Then he lunges at me.

But now I can stop him. With a wave of my arm, I freeze his leg. He can't move. I can see the panic in his eyes as he thrashes wildly at the ice to free himself from it. I can hear my heart throbbing apace, blood rushing through my body faster than the speed of light.

v (speed of light in air) = c/n

Where,

c (speed of light in vacuum) = 3 x 108 m/s

n (refractive index of air) = 1.0003

So,

Speed of light in air = 299702547.236 m/s

Kherun walks up to Bassam and asks, 'How did you find us, Bassam? Tell me ... Who all know that you are here?'

Bassam is shaking. Terrified.

'We put everyone ... we put all the Americans under surveillance. For their own protection ... and just in case ... just in case, you know ... if they were up to some mischief. We can trust no one.'

'What? Surveillance?' I yell. 'But we are *family*. We haven't seen you in over a decade and you think we are spies ... *traitors*?'

'We trust no one,' Bassam repeats like he's reading off a script.

Seriously, this guy must have been manufactured without a brain. Model, parroting extremist. But I feel a strange empathy for him. He understands no other reality. Bassam has been raised in hate and brainwashed from the day he was born. What else can I expect from someone who has only known bigotry, fear and extremism?

Bassam continues, 'My spies alerted me that you were being abducted. I came to save you from these traitors. I knew it was the Army of the Pure. They are traitors and the greatest nuisance to my father.'

'You are the traitors! You have destroyed my Khudir. You continue to destroy the word of my Allah,' Kherun says.

'Kherun, I need you to leave,' I say, choosing my words carefully. 'Get these people out. I will have to go back to the palace with my brother.' I raise my hand to silence her protests. 'For now.'

Kherun doesn't look happy with what I've proposed. Bassam looks relieved, probably because this means he gets to leave unharmed.

'I have to.' I repeat, seeing the reluctance in Kherun's eyes. 'My family ... I have to tell them what I know.'

Suddenly, a flash of lightning lights up the horizon. The tranquil sky transforms into a swirling mass and a violent cacophony rends the air. A dark figure shoots across the desert sky. I can't believe my eyes. It's a man, and he is flying. *Flying.* Hurtling towards us like an angry comet.

Who on earth is this?

The figure lands in front of us with a deafening thud. It is the Great Khan, a geometric-patterned shawl draped over his shoulders. I realize he is wearing the Chaddor. I sense the wave of terror that ripples through the gathering. Everyone has heard the rumours about dark magic and sorcery, but no one has seen the might of the Great Khan's powers on display.

Too much is happening too fast. All my senses are on high alert, trying to process everything at once.

The Khan's eyes are blazing. He is angry. *Very angry.*

He takes stock of the situation. His son and soldiers are trapped, incapacitated. His nostrils flare as he looks at the frozen, shattered weapons and, in an instant, the shards of ice are restored into whole weapons. With his next glance, he frees Bassam from the ice-lock and thereafter his frozen soldiers. The royal army speedily picks up their weapons. It has taken him no time to turn the tables on us.

'You hurt my son,' he bellows, addressing no one in particular. His eyes are flaming red coals. Ready to singe and burn at will. His soul has no mercy.

Finally, he turns to look at me. 'You ... you did this,' he hisses.

I look at the Great Khan. My father. Dad. Abba. Abbu.

Asshole.

Am I to give him the benefit of the doubt because he happens to be my father? I think not.

I say the only thing that makes sense to me at that moment. 'I'm your daughter.'

An eerie silence descends around us. Everyone waits with bated breath, eyes peeled. What will the Khan say? What will he do?

He looks at me. A moment of confusion in his eyes. Is that remorse I see on his face? Recognition? Love, perhaps? Then, without any warning, he directs a sharp bolt of lightning at me.

I block his attack with a wave of my hand that sends a jet of water towards his bolt. They meet mid-air in a terrific collision and both energies hold their own, refusing to back down.

What happens when an immovable object meets an unstoppable force? I guess we shall find out. Today. Here. Now.

He looks surprised. He didn't expect this. With a blood-curdling scream he attacks again. This time with more gusto. I have no option but to fight harder. I give it everything I have. My might, my will, my anger, my hurt. This is it. Do or die.

But deep down I know that I'm not that strong. I'm too new to this. I can feel the Khan's energy overpowering mine. I know I won't be able to hold him off much longer.

'Run! Get out of here,' I urge Kherun as I send fresh jets of water at the Khan. He ducks and sends another bolt of lightning towards me. I can only engage him for so long. 'Run, Kherun. Get your people to safety!'

Out of the corner of my eye I see Kherun finally comprehend. She hustles her crew to flee. 'Take care my child,' I hear her say. 'This is the beginning.'

I continue fighting the Khan's assaults as Kherun and her ragtag army proceed to escape.

My thoughts are pounding in my head. I don't understand it ... Even assholes have a soft corner for their children, yes? I'm his daughter. *I'm more than that annoying wedding guest from Amreeka.*

I continue to counter the Khan with every ounce of energy left in me. I send a last jet of water, the strongest I have generated thus far. But he squashes it easily with a flash of lightning from his eyes. With this last herculean effort, I collapse on the sandy ground.

There is only one thought swirling in my head: I don't wish to get up, ever again.

17

A Twist of Fate

May you have an *interesting life*. I have often wondered if that is a curse or a blessing.

Certainly, the past week has brought a lot of changes. History is going to remember this time long after we have turned to dust. Each day has brought us a new tale of interest, a fresh discovery and a different reason for anxiety. We are, so to speak, in the eye of the storm.

There is something about this girl. Zeba. She is always preoccupied. Brooding. Then laughing out loud. Brash. Saying things she does not mean. Trying to create some mischief.

But today, she sits attentively, brows knitted. Deep in thought, eyes boring into the chessboard. Her hands are in cuffs, making her movements clumsy. The Khan has put a pair of magical handcuffs on her to restrict her from using her powers. Or 'superpowers', as Zeba calls them.

So no water jets. No turning water into ice and back again. No way to escape. Zeba is powerless.

Yet, she does not cry. Does not shed a tear from sadness or frustration.

It took us a while to figure out that Allah has not granted her one of the things that make womankind such a force to reckon with. Their ability to let out their turmoil in torrents of tears. Tears help women return to their centre faster. The more turbulence a woman has seen, the more she has wept, and the stronger she has become. I have always believed that a woman truly finds herself in moments of utter weakness. Such a paradox!

But Zeba has not met that side of her. She has not met that moment. She has not met herself. Yet.

The girl has no outlet. I cannot imagine how she dealt with growing up. No tears during heartaches, through all the confusion of puberty ... People around her must have misunderstood her inability to cry for coldness or arrogance and treated her more harshly.

When she regained consciousness in the harem, at first Zeba screamed endlessly. Broke things in her room. Poured out her rage, anger, frustration.

I have seen this so many times in the past with so many others. She was not just angry; she was grieving. For her mother. For herself. For the lack of love and acceptance from her birth father. She was grieving about her life. I saw her move from denial to anger to depression to acceptance. Feeling it all too quickly, haphazardly.

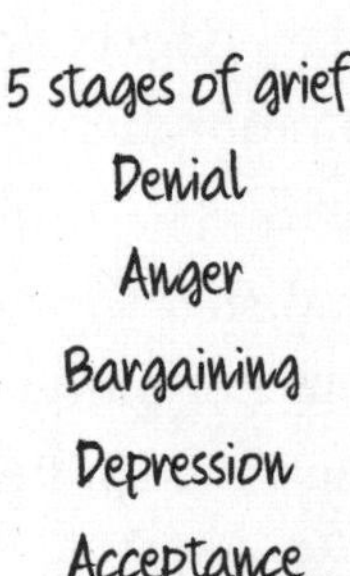

Surprisingly, she skipped the 'bargaining' stage altogether. Interesting child.

Her angry rants went on for a week. For a few days, she sulked and refused to eat. But then, eventually, she ventured out of her room and asked for a sandwich. Then she skulked and sauntered around till she discovered the games room and met BiBi.

BiBi is our great old dame. By all accounts, she is over a hundred years old. She speaks to no one—unless, that is, she has a vision. She is our cherished oracle who suffers from Alzheimer's and has great difficulty in recognizing common things. Yet, she can singularly focus on the chessboard placed in front of her.

Every day, BiBi sits in her favourite corner on her favourite chair, with her paan in her mouth and a silver spittoon by her side. Every hour, a hookah is made for her by her trusted aide, the eunuch Haya. She sits austerely in her corner, taking deep drags from her hookah, and plays chess all day long. By herself. Or Candy Crush on the new iPhone we got her with a beautiful, customized LV BiBi cover. She loves them, her phone and the game. Her obsession with it is legendary. Once, she played for four days straight and after that we had to ration her screen time.

She likes to be by herself and with herself. But the day Zeba walked over and silently watched BiBi play, something happened. BiBi looked up from her game and pointed her hookah pipe in Zeba's direction. She motioned at her to come, play. Zeba sat down and they played for the next two days. Not a word was exchanged between them. Every time one of them lost a pawn or captured the Queen, only small grunts or deep sighs could be heard.

I have been watching them play every day. BiBi, the never-moving ancient dame, and Zeba, the young novice, ever dynamic, untameable.

Oh, but why does this girl slouch so much! I tap her on the shoulder and say, 'Sit up!'

She looks up at me from the chessboard and blinks.

'Be an exclamation mark. Not a question mark,' I say firmly.

I remember my mother saying this to me when I was six. Ever since then, the words have been in my head every walking and sitting moment. I doubt Zeba will ever stop slouching. But if she is to look inwards and find her centre, she must focus her attention on her body first and straighten her spine.

I think I see a flicker of a smile on her face. Perhaps of acceptance. Is she enjoying her time with BiBi, enjoying being here? Then, suddenly, a dark cloud passes over her face. Her eyes change colour. And she turns her face away to focus on the chessboard.

I gather it is guilt she is feeling. Umar and his family have been chained and thrown into captivity by the Khan, and Zeba has been sent to the harem. She is the Khan's daughter, after all. He sent word that he wants to raise his daughter as a 'proper woman'. She must be re-programmed and married off soon, in adherence to the rules of the land. I wanted to tell her that this seemingly awful fate might be the best thing that could have happened to her. But I held my tongue.

Among the many things my mother used to say, one of her favourites was: **Speak less, observe more.** When I started heeding her advice, every time I wanted to say something, I would pause to consider if it was a thought or words that came from my inner core. I found over the years that I had less and less to say. And more and more to observe. Eventually, I only said what really had to be said. Nothing more, nothing less. My conversations and observations became granular and talking became an organic process. I no longer felt the need to chatter away or indulge in loose gossip or plan idly for the future.

I watch now as Zeba takes out BiBi's bishop. The old dame grunts in annoyance. Zeba cheekily gestures a win.

I smile. Perhaps Zeba really is beginning to feel comfortable here.

You see, staying in the North Wing of the palace, where she was earlier, means you are away from all the action on this side. The North Wing is a sanctified part of the palace, reserved for guests who either do not stay too long or have to be impressed. It is far from the West Wing of the palace, where the harem is located. The women's-only section. A water garden separates us from the rest of the palace and special permissions are needed to enter the harem. It is an oasis, a world apart.

My thoughts are interrupted by BiBi's grunt as she gets up suddenly and walks away from the chessboard. This abrupt departure leaves Zeba clueless and alone, staring at the chess pieces. She holds the fallen bishop regretfully between two fingers. This game was her only escape. Now the daunting task of her future actions will press on more urgently.

As she stares outside the window, broodingly she states, 'I need to save my family. They are in captivity because of me.' I look up. She is regarding me with piercing eyes. Her voice is low, her face impassive. 'I got them into this, and I will get them out.'

Of course, I want to say, what is your plan? But I do not say anything.

Zeba looks away and lowers her head. She knows, as I do, that there is no plan.

I was anticipating this. Now is the right time to show her everything.

'Come,' I say, beckoning her to follow me.

I lead her to the far end of the West Wing and then down a flight of stairs towards the dungeon where the female tailors and seamstresses have their workstations. We need a lot of abayas and veils for different days of the week, and then there are the ceremonies, christenings, births, deaths and royal visits, so this section of the palace is always hard at work. Apart from just abayas, they also stitch day wear, summer dresses, winter shawls, nightwear. And when the harem women indulge in online shopping (which is quite often), alter, restitch and sometimes even redesign garments to specifications.

This is the busiest area in all of the West Wing.

Zeba's eyes widen as she walks behind me, gaping at the rows of workers toiling tirelessly, almost in unison. It is our mini factory under the West Wing. A world that she has not seen and did not know existed. I guess, like many others I know, she too assumed that her custom-made clothes came out of thin air.

We walk briskly into the royal cloth room. Rolls upon rolls of fabric line the room in long columns on long perpendicular racks that stretch right up to the high ceiling. This is my favourite room. The rolls of cloth are stacked in beautiful symmetry. Coded by colour. The darkest shade at the bottom and the lightest at the top. Each column a work of art. In fact, the whole room is a work of art. It reflects perfect order in a seemingly chaotic world. It is my sanctuary.

With Zeba scurrying along behind me, I stride over to the blue column, stacked neatly between the pink and purple ones. A ceiling-high column of cloth in all the possible shades of blue. Turquoise, Powder, Sky, Electric Air Force, Baby Blue, Tiffany, Steel, Carolina, Turkish Blue, Pigeon, Maya, Teal, Independence, Cornflower, Olympic. Sapphire, Azure, Egyptian, Yale, Navy, Prussian, Space, Royal.

We walk past the blue column and towards the red. I move the column to the right and then pull it forward—a movement not possible to replicate in any other row or column of this room. Behind the red column, a secret passage reveals itself.

I turn to look at Zeba. Her jaw has dropped.

Now I feel I must say something. 'Welcome to the harem,' I say.

There are so many tales and fables about what life in a harem is like. Many travellers and writers have attempted to write about it. There are several wild accounts of how many women live there, and the imaginary and inflated sexual escapades of the King.

The inner workings of harem life continue to capture the imagination of the world. And though this is a space wholly run by women, the Harem Mistress and guards, eunuchs who are privy to everything inside, where no man has ever been allowed to enter, it has always only been the men who have written and talked about the life inside. Without going into specifics, I can confidently say that all of these so-called accounts and histories are inaccurate. So today I shall tell you, as I tell Zeba, the truth about life in the harem. My own lived experience.

The harem refers to that area of the Khan's household that belongs to the women. A perfectly sealed sanctuary to which the outside world, everyone other than its inhabitants, has no access. The harem includes the living quarters of the Khan's wives, his daughters, female servants, eunuchs and slaves. It would have housed his mother and sisters too had they been alive. But they had passed away years ago.

Yes, it also houses his concubines. But this is not what defines the harem; it is only one part of it. The section where new entrants to the harem are housed is called Husna Home. But, honestly, the Khan's ability in the bedroom in the last decade has been ... what is that dirty line? ... more talk and less c@#k. One night, one of the naughty ones emptied out his vial of Viagra and replaced it with calcium tablets, causing the Khan to leave very quickly, red-faced and in a huff. How these wicked women squealed with laughter. The embarrassed Khan seldom visits now, which gives the women more freedom to do what they please.

You see, the harem was designed keeping in mind the Khan's rigid interpretation of the very strict Sharia Law. Be watched closely and kept veiled. But the women of the harem are no mute spectators. We have fought back over the years, every chance we have got. The confines of the harem thus became the one place where the handful of us were free. The women within the harem are the only free people in Khudir. It never occurred to the Khan that he was creating right under his nose a perfect sanctuary for us. A household within the palace. With no interference from the Khan himself. A place where we are free to do whatever we please in the company of other women. Most of us are educated. We read, study, play chess, sing, dance, entertain each other.

And here, in this hidden portion, lies another world. An office. A long line of cubicles stocked with state-of-the-art computers and satellite phones. Women running around with files and making calls. The only non-office elements are the beautiful rugs, a gigantic coffee and snack bar, and high-backed comfortable chairs upholstered in beautiful floral textiles. The office is busy and chaotic but not without dollops of feminine aesthetic touches.

A lot of important work happens here. You see, this secret chamber hidden behind the column of red materials in the giant haberdashery is the main base of the Resistance. From here, we help smuggle young girls who are forcibly abducted by the Khan out of Khudir. We get fake passports made for them. Write to embassies and get them asylum, help them enrol in universities in far corners of the world. Even get some of them married. We have formed political alliances and are in touch with Female Resistance Movements across the world and they help us in our collective fight.

'So, the harem women do what they want to with multitudes of servants serving them all day and all of the Khan's resources at their beck and call?' Zeba remarks, a note of awe creeping into her voice.

'Yes, in a way. This is our empire, and we run it. We also try and influence what goes on in the outside world. We help in securely and secretly housing refugees, especially women who are being persecuted and no longer have a home.'

'And the men? What about men who are persecuted?' Zeba asked.

'Only women are allowed inside the harem. But we help whoever we can. We help everyone.'

'And the children born here?'

'All children born in the harem are raised by collectively by us. The West Wing has nurseries, play pens, classrooms, activity areas, and an exhaustive library for young minds. The boys remain in the harem until puberty, after which they move into the King's South Wing.'

Zeba was listening intently, and I continued, 'With so many young boys with a potential claim to the throne, there is always a lot of rivalry and jealousy in the South Wing. They are constantly scrambling to be the Khan's favourite son. But the Khan has chosen his heir. Bassam. His soul is as dark as the Khan's ...' I paused, my mind flooded with thoughts.

In my opinion, the rightful heir to Khudir's throne is our kind-hearted Sayed. What a beautiful empathetic boy he has grown up to be. He is not my son. But he is a joy to all of us in the harem. Generous, thoughtful, compassionate. He has not forgotten his mothers and sisters in the harem. If he becomes King, there will be no nation as great as Khudir. No people happier or better taken care of. We have to make that happen. Sayed must succeed to the throne. Bassam cannot be King.

So much to do. So much to share with this girl ...

I look at Zeba. This is the first time she has truly met the women of the harem. Seen us for what we are—strong, smart, educated, independent-minded women with individual identities. We are more than just our veils. We may be spoken of as the invisible ones. But we have always been in plain sight. Behind our hijabs we are all fighters. Soldiers of a silent revolution, in our own way.

I tell her about our secret chant. Our silent pact. Our foundation that remains unbroken. No matter what.

I am your daughter. Your sister.
Together we fight.
Together we prevail.

She is quiet, impassive. Allah! This girl is a tough nut to crack.

'Come. You have a visitor,' I say. She nods, gesturing that I should proceed.

Zeba and I walk out to the secret garden beyond the office.

There, alone on a bench, sits Kherun, her optimistic smile making her face glow.

18

Miriam's Grave

'How do you know which one is my mother's?' asked Zeba.

Zeba and Kherun were walking in an old graveyard, and the long line of unmarked graves seemed endless.

'I do not,' said Kherun.

Zeba stopped in her tracks.

Kherun continued, 'Honestly, I have forgotten. It has been so many years and her final resting place was not marked by a tombstone. But one night in a dream I saw you walk with me to a particular grave. And you put a single white lily on this grave and said, "This is my mother. My Ammi." I came here the very next day, and knew instinctively that my vision, my dream, was correct. It was certainly Miriam's final resting place.'

'Great,' said Zeba sarcastically. 'You made me sneak out of the palace for a hunch based on a dream. Just great.'

'I know you are finding much of what is happening difficult to believe. Unfathomable. But trust me, it is all ...'

'Of course, it's all true. I was shooting killer water jets from my hands till a few days ago. And now my own father has put me in these,'—she gestures at her bonded wrists—'these ... golden handcuffs and my powers have just dried up. Unbelievable! Un-fucking-possible! Who am I kidding? I don't even *really* know who I am. Daughter of an evil wizard? Bastard child of an abducted teenage mother? Freak? Who the fuck am I?'

Zeba's voice echoed in the empty graveyard. An ancient owl stared at them from atop a lone tree.

Kherun said, 'You are indeed all these things. And none of them. You are you. You are Zeba. You, dear girl, may be a product of your circumstances. But you are not their prisoner. The past is very clever, my child. It sneaks up on you and snares you. Do not let your past trap you.'

'Just take me to ... it. To her,' Zeba said. She was clearly in no mood for conversation, much less a philosophical one.

The owl hooted knowingly as the two made their way to Miriam's grave.

A strong gust of wind blew. Their black hijabs fluttered in the wind. Zeba was wearing a hijab for the first time in her life and she hated it. But she knew she had no choice. They had to be careful while sneaking out of the heavily guarded West Wing. These nondescript black hijabs, usually worn by female staff members of the harem, helped them move undetected. Zeba tugged at her hijab uncomfortably, muttering under her breath. Kherun shook her head but said nothing.

Kherun and the Sultana had waited for the longest time for Zeba to arrive in Khudir. After running this silent revolution for so many years, it had seemed to them that Zeba was their last remaining hope. But it worried them, how unprepared she seemed for such a big responsibility.

She had no idea what to do, or how to save herself, let alone all of Khudir. The lines on Kherun's face deepened even as a thought flickered across her mind. *Is Zeba really the saviour we have been waiting for? Allah reham.*

Kherun knew that Zeba was feeling just as short-changed and unhappy as she was at this moment. They shared only a sense of misery as common ground. Kherun stopped beside an unmarked grave with weeds growing all over it and looked meaningfully at Zeba. She closed her eyes, cupped her hand and said a prayer for the departed.

Inna Illahi Wa Inna Ilayhi Raji'un

Then she stepped back, letting Zeba be alone.

Zeba looked at the grave. It was just a mound of dirt and weeds. But as she sat down next to it, her heart began pounding. Her knees felt weak. Her body went numb. She touched the cracked mud of the grave the way she would have liked to hold her mother's hand. She caressed the weeds as if stroking her mother's soft dark hair.

The sky grew darker and thunder rumbled in the distance, as it started to rain. Yet, Zeba remained still, sitting, her head bowed. Drenching herself in the rain. The sadness that had weighed her down her whole life hit her now like a tonne of bricks, a whole house collapsing on her head. Throughout her life, Zeba had never been able to cry. It didn't matter how sad or upset or angry she felt, or how alone and heartbroken, not a single tear would emerge from her eyes. *Non-functional tear glands*—that's all she ever heard. Today, as she sat alone next to her mother's grave, rain pelting down on her, Zeba shed tears for the very first time. She cried, inconsolably, deep sobs racking her body. Then she lay down next to where her mother lay, curled up, like a child in the womb. She wept, and the heavens wept with her.

The women in the harem had taught Zeba a prayer—an old Arabic prayer for the soul of the departed. She muttered it now, forgetting half the words, mispronouncing many. But her intention was pure, and they say intention is nobler than memory.

Niyat.

So it didn't really matter.

Finally, exhausted, she closed her eyes and drifted into a dream. A kind of a vision ... Or did it really happen? We shall never know, but to Zeba it was every bit as real as anything had ever been.

She saw herself sitting on a beautiful green hill looking out at a pleasant sky. She saw a herd of goats being herded by a small boy with a long stick. The goats were peacefully grazing on the mountainside, while the boy sat nearby, bored, chewing on a piece of fruit. The green hill was littered with small pellet-like goat droppings.

'He has another hour before the sun goes down and he takes his goats home,' she heard someone say.

Zeba turned around. A young girl was standing behind her. She looked happy, dressed in a traditional dress made of a beautiful shimmery grey. She patted Zeba's cheek and smiled. 'Do you know who I am?' she asked.

Zeba nodded, the answer coming to her instinctively. Miriam looked like a teenager. Barely a child. More than a decade younger than Zeba was now. Zeba wanted to say 'Mother ... Ammi ...' Something. Unable to find the words, she just nodded.

What would Miriam have liked to be called? What do you call your dead mother's ghost? Zeba wasn't sure. There was no precedent for it anywhere in the world.

Miriam kept talking. Her voice was of a young girl's, but her words had the maturity of an old soul.

'Do you know how I died? Kherun must have told you.'

Zeba nodded.

'But you don't know why ...'

Zeba felt an anxiety growing within her. *What does she mean, 'why'?*

'I was a goatherd's daughter. Plucked out of school, taken from my family. Unknown to me, I was made to participate in a dark magic ritual. The Blood Ritual. The Khan didn't desire me. You see, his harem is not about lust. He was invoking a very old spell. Ancient magic. One that involved human sacrifice. All of it to access the power of Yazoo.'

Zeba was stunned.

'I know you used to think that Yazoo is just a story. But perhaps now you have changed your mind? Magic is all around us. Even in everyday life. It's always there, whether you want to see it or not. But dark magic is dangerous. It makes people do the worst deeds for power and glory. The Khan wanted to be the King of the World, and for that he was willing to go to any lengths. Nothing would stop him. He was ready to invoke the darkest force known to humanity: Yazoo, the messenger of Shaitan. The ultimate darkness. Yazoo had been banished millennia ago to the underbelly of the Earth. He lay there, dormant. To awaken this evil force, the Khan needed to do a special kind of ancient dark magic. One that needed human blood. *The blood of one hundred and one virgins and their first-born children*. An ancient and dangerous spell.

'The Khan handpicked one hundred and one virgins from all over Khudir. He had to impregnate these young girls on the first moon of the month. He kidnapped the poor girls from their homes; took them away from their families. They were kept in the harem till they bore him a child. Then he took a vial of the blood of his hundred and one wives and their firstborns to complete his spell to invoke Yazoo.'

Zeba felt the horror of the King's deeds. 'He k-k-killed them all?' she stammered.

'Thankfully, no. He just needed some blood. A vial of it. After which, most of them were sent back to the streets. The infant boys were kept, of course. The infant girls were abandoned on sidewalks and street corners. Many of the harem girls never went back to their families after the Khan threw them out. They died of hunger or went mad or killed themselves. But as the spell progressed, the Khan became stronger and stronger. He was well on his way to being the most powerful man in the world. You, my Zeba, were the last one. You were the last child. With your blood, he would finally fulfil his dark desire. To rule the world.'

Miriam's eyes lingered on Zeba, her expression a mix of nostalgia and pain. 'But I overheard him talking to one of his trusted cronies. I knew that your blood was the last thing he needed for his evil plans to succeed. The night I started getting contractions prematurely, I knew you were coming. You were early by a month and a half. It was the will of Allah. Thankfully, the Khan was not in Khudir. I had to make a terrible choice. Save your life or save the world.'

Miriam paused. The she looked at Zeba and asked, 'Do you think I did the right thing?'

After a long silence, Zeba said quietly, 'Yes, you did the right thing.'

Miriam held her hand. 'He already had my blood in his possession, but I could not let him get his hands on yours. I decided to sacrifice your life to save Khudir, to save all of humanity. You stopped the Khan. You stopped Yazoo. Your death made sure his evil plans never unfolded ...'

Miriam broke down.

'I know you must hate me. But what has happened has happened. There is no point in holding a grudge against a ghost.'

'Are you a ghost?'

'What do you think?'

'I don't think ... you're a ... ghost.'

Miriam smiled.

'And I don't hate you. You are my mother ...'

'You are brave, my Zeba. Your whole life you have struggled with questions about why your parents abandoned you. Well, you finally have the truth. You were not rejected. You are, in fact, the chosen one. Chosen to make the ultimate sacrifice. To stop the evil Khan. You were chosen by the holy Zsa Zsa to be saved. You were always the chosen one, my child.'

'Weren't you scared ... doing what you did?' Zeba asked.

'I had seen the Khan do such awful things that it shook my heart. After I died, he was never able to resurrect Yazoo, and it stopped him in his tracks. He tried many more times, with many other children, but it didn't work. No other child's blood would work because my blood had already been offered to Yazoo. It had to be yours. When the spell didn't work, it made the Khan even more angry. He killed many innocents in his rage ... even some of his own children. But it put an end to his larger evil design. Your life to save the world. That's the choice ... the sacrifice I had to make. But see the miracles of all miracles, Zsa Zsa saved you, kept you alive and safe, far away.'

'But ... why me?'

'Because ... I just told you ... you were the child conceived last ... the hundred and first ...'

'Nooo ... why *me*? Why did Zsa Zsa save *me*?'

Miriam smiles kindly. 'You may be the Khan's daughter, but you are blessed with the power of your mother's love, sacrifice and innocence. You have all of me. Zsa Zsa chose to save you to bring peace into this cruel and hateful world. *Whenever darkness threatens to take over the world a saviour appears. To restore equilibrium.* Now the choice is yours

... what will you do? Now that you know everything. Now that you have seen it all.'

Zeba held her mother's hand as tears flowed down her face. Miriam kissed her forehead gently.

Gestures often have unbelievable and undeniable powers unknown to us. And pure acts of love have the power to change the future of the world. This was that moment.

Her mother's kiss caused the gold handcuffs on Zeba's wrists to lose their power. They slid off, leaving her free.

Miracle #5 ... or is it #4? Sorry, I've lost count, dear reader. Our story has quite a few of them.

That day, Zeba realized who she really was. That day, Miriam showed Zeba her true path: to save all of mankind from war and hatred. That day, the superpowers given to Zeba found a purpose. A meaning.

The rain stopped and the clouds parted. The sun smiled brightly again.

Zeba opened her eyes. A sudden gust of wind and her black hijab fluttered, majestically. Magically.

The hijab ... it no longer felt oppressive and stifling to Zeba. In fact, it flew around her and flapped about with unmatched elegance. Zeba could feel this new hijab becoming her new identity. Forged out of her, for her. It gave her a sense of autonomy, safety, power and—most importantly for a superhero—the gift of anonymity.

Zeba felt the hijab become her shield against the world, the true expression of her superpowers, her superhero cape! She knew now that the fight was not against one man or to avenge one death. It was a fight *for* freedom. Not just for herself or for the Akhoon family. For to fight for mere personal gain or revenge would shame the sacrifices of all the women and men who came before her.

As she stood in all her might and glory, Zeba saw herself clearly: a warrior standing on the shoulders of the giants who came before her. People who put the greater good above their own interests. She must honour their sacrifice. *Must fight.*

And so, at her mother's old unmarked grave, Zeba was introduced to her identity and purpose: **To save the world from the Khan.**

Music rises to thunderous crescendo OR
a Zeba theme music kicks in.

For future film costume departments attempting to create the 'Zeba Hijab Superhero Outfit', please make the black look slick. The vibe can become a bit too typical, attract attention. Look tacky in the wrong light. Let's find a balance between looking wholesome and fashionable. Reference, Chris Nolan's Batman costume. Gal Gadot's in Wonder Woman was good, too. A bit of sexiness never killed anyone. No skin, but modest chic perhaps? Good makeup ... strong highlighter and contours. Let the eyes do the talking.

19

The Khan Goes All In

Bitch! She thinks she can undo years of hard work, toil and planning?

I am the son of Zahid the Benevolent. I hail from the great unbroken line of the Akhoons, and she thinks she can walk in here and defeat me? She thinks she can learn dark magic in one day?

Hahaha!

I have worked hard and waited. Every single day.

I never gave up. Never.

Ever since my Blood Ritual spell backfired, I have not been able to fuck a woman in peace. It was all about getting my blood heir. I would have happily fucked every virginal bitch in Khudir till they gave me a child whose blood would invoke Yazoo. But it just did not happen.

Last time, my plan had failed. But not this time.

The Akhoons were the last keepers of the secrets of the dark world. I have studied these secrets for years. Now, this bitch has left me no option. I know what must be done.

I have to initiate the Last Spell.

Akhir.

It is the most difficult spell known to the Akhoons. Many have tried to erase even the memory of this spell. Because it is rumoured to be so evil.

Idiots.

Did they not know that trying to hide something makes it even more desirable? And true seekers like me always find ways to unearth forbidden things from the forgotten pages of history. I have found an old parchment from Antiquity that contains the spell to invoke Yazoo. At a supposedly terrible cost—the soul of the person casting the spell. There is no coming back from it. Once cast, Yazoo will rise and I will become a little less human. Have a little less of a soul.

My soul. My rooh.

Bah! So what? It may matter to some, but not to me. A small price to pay if you ask me.

I will be ruler of the world. What will I do with my soul? Kings have no need for that sort of stuff. In any case, magic is magic. It is meant to help one achieve one's goal. There is no right or wrong in magic. I must give up something in order to get what I want. That is just how the world works. So, yes, I am happy to give up half of my soul to Yazoo to invoke him, to control the world. Bring back ORDER. Dismantle this disease called Democracy.

My plan is set.

For years I have funded **the Royal Global Research Team** to find and track down all the erstwhile world leaders—monarchs and kings who no longer rule, and their heirs. The R.G.R.T. found bloodlines of the real leaders and kings of the world. The last King in Mongolia was found working as a blacksmith, a bloody blacksmith! Another King from Ahuda, a province in India, is an actor in Bollywood, singing and dancing to earn a living, his palace converted into a hotel for foreign tourists. RK, Raees Khan—such a loser. I shall unite them all under my tutelage. I will free this world of Democracy. And then I will be King of the New World.

All men are not created equal. Some lives are more important than others. More precious. Maybe women can all be equal—equally useful for serving and servicing men's needs. Still, even among them, some are definitely more of use than others. Regardless, they must be made to toe the line. Young and old. Royal and plebeian.

That old hag BiBi, who pretends to be an oracle, once told me that I will never be King of the World. BiBi, the bloody bitch. If she really was a true oracle, would she not have a life better than the one she does now as a prisoner? I will keep that old whore alive till she sees me crowned the Emperor of the World. Master of All. Master of Yazoo.

Hahaha.

Yazoo. The ancient books describe him as a fabled one-eyed monster who can gulp down oceans in one sip and still be thirsty for more. He can generate so much heat that the Sun would pale in comparison. He can control all energy sources and fresh water sources. All weapons, including those that rely on nuclear energy. His powers are greater than anything ever known to man.

But the best power of all? The ability to take the form of your biggest weakness, your greatest fear. He gets inside your head and weakens you. No man, no woman can ever be a match for the might of this dark force.

This Kingdom of Khudir is my jaan, but I want more. I want the entire world to be my throne and footstool. Everyone should bow to my commands.

The time has come.

I do not even have to kill everyone. I will simply have Yazoo control all the water and nuclear energy of the world. Every country, every leader will bow down to me. The world will be at my mercy. Then I will summon my R.G.R.T. and I will appoint the **lost kings and monarchs** as chieftains all over the globe. The Mongolian blacksmith shall reclaim what is his. The Russian baker will be Tsar again. The Indian actor will be Sultan once more. The world will be cut up like a big juicy melon, one that I can eat at my fancy and spit the seeds out. Democratic armies and secret service agents from across the world can try and stop me, but I will crush them like flies. They will try and launch an attack. But they do not truly understand the enemy. They do not know me. They do not know Yazoo. They are going to walk into an ambush. It will be my delight and pleasure to crush them.

My mind is restless.

It has been two weeks since that American girl tried to take me down. Two weeks since I have been holed up in the Magic Caves of Khudir wearing just a loincloth, performing this long arduous magic spell. No fancy robes, no jewels, not even my Chaddor. This magic spell must be performed without any material possessions.

I have told my soldiers and Bassam to leave me alone. In my absence, my son will take care of the kingdom. At last, it is time for my tete-a-tete with Yazoo.

I had this choice years ago too, but I was afraid then. I could not muster up the courage to offer my soul to Yazoo. I know this magic is dangerous and almost impossible to reverse. Many have attempted this and lost their lives in the bargain. But I am no longer afraid. My only desire is to fulfil my childhood dream of ruling the world. And I shall brook no opposition. Today, I am going to perform the last spell. The final act.

The cauldron bubbles with potent magical ingredients before me. I raise the royal sword and cut my left hand. A drop of blood falls into the boiling cauldron.

I AM ALL IN.

There is no turning back now.

20

Dark Night of the Soul

One would think that it is not such a big deal. After all, the Khan does not have much to offer by way of his soul anyway, right? All that is left of his soul is a mouldy black rotting little piece. What could he possibly get in exchange for that?

Right?

Well, wrong, apparently.

Despite the riches the Khan had accumulated over the years, it seems the only thing he really truly possessed was his soul. The only part of himself that lasted beyond his body. Forever.

So then, who was the Khan without his soul?

An empty shell, that's what, which only just looks like a human body. Numb to all sensation, unfeeling, unloving, yet constantly hungry, for chaos, for power. An obsessive abomination fully controlled by Yazoo. There was just one thing on his mind, a phrase he kept muttering like a mantra. *King of the world! King of the world*! Straight out of a fan-made trailer of *Titanic*.

In a way he was no longer the Khan. He had been reduced to a vegetable. A big unsavoury pumpkin rotting from the inside after its magic Cinderella-hour ran out and it was discarded, not even considered good enough to be stuffed as decoration at a salad bar or carved into a lousy Halloween lantern.

The only bit of him that harked back to the man he had been was a single memory. It was of his childhood, of the genesis of his journey to becoming the monstrous being he was today. The memory was of the most important day in Khudir's history: the **Black Day**, when he was a little boy about to undertake a gruelling walk.

Let's start at the beginning. In a time long past, which was a simple time, a simpler Khudir was ruled by the kind and just King Zahid, simply called Shah by his newly united kingdom. There were no oil wells or big cities or airports in Khudir, but there was peace. This lasted until first the Russians and later the Americans came along.

The world was in the throes of the Cold War era; Khudir was but a tiny kingdom that lay in the path of a hungry Russia. The threat of a mega power like Russia attacking Khudir and taking over all its villages loomed large. For the people of Khudir, scarier than losing their land was the possibility of a foreign power taking away their identity, religion and culture.

No God? No Allah? It was unthinkable.

The Americans, on the other hand, arrived in Khudir with their candy, charisma, saccharine smiles and promises of saving the land. They supplied the Akhoon leader, the First King of Khudir, Zahid the Benevolent, with guns and ammunition and made promises of protecting his kingdom from the Russians. The CIA used the young Khan's brothers and half-brothers as undercover operatives to collect data against Russia and keep an eye on the movements of their troops.

But there always comes a time when tenuous friendships get tested. And when that hour dawned, when the ancient tribes of Khudir really needed protection, the Americans turned their backs on a whole population. It was too risky. Khudir was not *that* important. It was not *their* war.

Villages and cities across the entire Kingdom of Khudir were bombed. The royal family was almost annihilated. The only survivors were Zahid's bastard son, the boy Khan, and his four-year-old half-brother, Umar. They lived, saved by an old cook who hid them in the basement of the newly constructed unpretentious palace of Zahid the Benevolent.

After the explosions halted, the old cook tunnelled both the brothers out to safety. As the young Khan stepped out and looked at the bombed-out palace, he held his step-brother to his chest, trying to soothe him even as bitter tears rolled down his own cheeks. He heard a groan, a familiar voice, and rushed to see who lay in the rubble that was once their home, their humble palace. There he found his father, the First King of Khudir, trapped under piles of bricks and smashed concrete. Only his head was visible through some gaps in the rubble.

The boy yelled for help, frantically digging through the rubble with his bare hands.

'SHAH! SHAH! SHAH!'

A few remaining shattered survivors heard him calling out to Shah—the name that Zahid the Benevolent was affectionately known by—and cautiously came out of their hiding places to help the young Khan. *Maybe there is hope,* they thought. *Maybe something of the kingdom could be saved after all. All will be well if our King is alive.*

Finally, after two hours of digging, they managed to free the King. But the person whom they rescued from under the pile of rubble was no longer the King they had known. He was half gone. *Literally.*

Zahid the Benevolent had lost both his arms and legs and had been reduced to a stump. Barely alive, the King managed somehow to instruct his son to take him to a nearby tribal town that may have escaped being bombed because it was situated in the cover of a looming hill. The young Khan handed his little brother Umar to a kind woman. The Shah's followers pointed the Khan to an abandoned old bull cart and the young boy reverently placed King Zahid on it. With no beast of burden in sight, he dragged the cart himself until they reached their destination. The rest of the few hundred survivors grabbed whatever they could get their hands on in the mad rush to get to safety. Money, jewellery, family heirlooms, furniture, utensils, livestock, food and water. Then they left the village forever, following in the Khan's footsteps.

This day went down in Khudir's history as the **Black Day**, and young Khan's journey to safety the **Hijr of Shah**.

Take a moment dear reader, for an interesting exercise.

Ask yourself this: What is the one thing you will take before running out of your house in case of a fire, or flood, or war? What is that one thing you would tuck under your arm or lift over your head or hide under your coat? What would you take with you if you had to leave overnight?

Money? Passports? Keys to your house for when you can return? A lover's old shirt? A dead man's bones in an urn? An iPhone charger? A bottle of rum? A photograph? Your diary?

You see, one can tell a lot about a person by the prized possession they reach for at a terrifying time like this. I would like you to truly know and acknowledge that authentic aspect of you. In short, you are what you grab. (Apologies if that sounds totally inappropriate.)

But to come back to the story at hand ... The Hijr of Shah was a quiet sad walk of defeat and desolation. No one uttered a single word. Yet their bodies, faces and possessions conveyed their violent story. The journey seemed never-ending as they walked. Hope evaporated and exhaustion set in and, one by one, they abandoned their beloved possessions by the side of the mountain. The longer they walked, the less important some of the things they had salvaged seemed. Still, they were poor people and having to discard their few earthly possessions broke their hearts.

When the sun rose high in the sky, the mountainside looked like a forlorn scrapyard. The boy Khan carried on, pulling the cart with all his might. He hardened his heart. He knew he had to avenge the misfortune that had befallen his people and his family. In particular, his father who had been a just and fair ruler of his people.

When they reached their destination, the young Khan took a moment to recover and catch his breath. Tears of pain and gratitude seeping from his eyes, King Zahid smiled at his son. He was close to death. But before drawing his last breath, he declared the young Khan as his successor.

Thus, at a tender age, the young Khan found himself burdened with heavy responsibilities. His younger brother to take care of. The fractured Kingdom of Khudir to lead and rebuild. He vowed that one day he would avenge his father's death. He would stab the Americans in their chests just as they had stabbed his family in the back. *Traitors.*

Friends who didn't honour their word. They were scumbags of a different order.

'Down with America! Bring down the infidels!' This became his daily chant.

In a way, the Khan was a monster created by the atrocities of an unjust world. He too started out as someone who suffered due to man's greed and utterly selfish nature.

Sadly, and unfortunately as is often the case, he became exactly like the people he hated. In fact, he became even more vile and evil than those he set out to destroy.

Now, reduced to nothingness by Yazoo, the Khan's decaying brain conjures up images of that long walk. The Hijr of Shah. In his mind's eye he sees a red whistle. Among the group that had set off on the long, arduous, seemingly endless walk alongside the Khan on **Black Day** was an old man who had a red whistle.

Throughout the journey, the man kept blowing on this red whistle.

One more step. One more whistle. One more step. One more whistle.
FWEET. FWEET. FWEET.

It became their marching beat.

After all these years, today, as the Khan utters his final wish and bargains away his soul to quell the fire of his lifelong hate against the enemy, this journey undertaken more than fifty years ago is the last memory that lingers in his fading mind. Of a little boy lugging his father's mutilated remains to safety on a barren mountainside.

That day, hate had reared its ugly head and left its indelible footprint. That day, hate had won and marked the soul of a little boy.

And, today, hate and Yazoo have won again.

The mighty Khan is reduced to a wide-eyed whistling idiot whose eyes will never leave the sight of Yazoo. For, to the Khan, Yazoo will appear for all eternity as the bloody stump of his dead father—Zahid the Benevolent.

Nothing could be a bigger punishment, a more horrifying consequence. Imagine being trapped in your worst nightmare, where you cannot tear your eyes away from the one image that you fear the most in the world. Doomed forever to keep muttering that one wish for which you gave up your soul: KING OF THE WORLD.

FWEET.

In this world or any other, there is nothing more valuable than a person's soul. To trade that away is the epitome of foolishness.

The blackened, sick soul of the Khan was worth a lot to Yazoo. But the Khan made a poor bargain. Indeed, he would sit on a throne. He would be King. In a twisted way, he would get his wish.

KING OF THE WORLD.

FWEET. FWEET.

Yazoo, appearing as the half-dead stump of Zahid to the crazed Khan, thundered, 'Bassam! Soldiers! Call for a carriage for the Khan, the New King of the World. Ha ha ha!'

21

Victory

When I see my daughter again, she is no longer just my daughter. She has become something ... *more.*

She has become a saviour.

Alhamdulillah.

I cannot believe the words as they are forming in my head. My Zeba, a saviour?

I can run from one pillar of this Great Hall to another screaming with joy. My daughter, a saviour! It sounds strange ... and so blessed.

Praise the lord.

Allah hu Akbar.

Honestly, I think all mothers secretly dream that their children will grow up to 'save the world' or hold the post of President, perhaps. If not of a great nation of the world, then of the Rotary Club or Lions Club at the least. As if just being happy or healthy is not good enough. What is the point of producing children if they cannot make you look good in front of the neighbours? It is all about legacy at the end of the day, is it not?

My Zeba. My prodigal daughter. She has, in a matter of hours, turned everything around.

The last few weeks have been a living hell. I thought I would never see her again. I was convinced we were all going to die here in Khudir. After the Khan captured Zeba and banished her to the harem, the wedding festivities were cut short. All the guests were ordered to leave the country immediately. There was panic everywhere. But my Umar was never one to take tyranny lying down. He stood up to the Khan and demanded that he set Zeba free. It was only right, he said, that our family be allowed to return home together.

'Home? That foreign country?' sneered the Khan. 'You have become the curse and the nuisance of my life, Umar. I loved you, protected you ... but you have always hated me. Why is that? You even took *my offspring* into your protection. You knew I needed her blood for the Blood Ritual, so you planned this. I should have killed you years ago, the day Baba died.'

I could hear defiance in Umar's voice when he replied, 'The fault is mine, Bhai. I should have stopped you years ago when I had the chance ... at least I would not have to watch my brother turn into a devil.' He spat on the ground before the Khan.

My husband and his brother ... two men who despise each other and are yet bonded by blood and childhood trauma.

'Go ahead then. Kill me!' Umar taunted the Khan. 'It is so easy for you to take a human life. Kill me with one strike. Finish it off. What are you waiting for?'

I cried out to Umar to stop, to step back. But he was adamant.

'My children, Ayesha and I are going to go home,' he continued. 'I am sure you do not want your American friends to find out what you are doing here. One call to the Embassy. All I have to say is that my crazy brother is keeping my family hostage here. Do not make me do that.'

'UMAR!' the Khan roared, and I saw a bright bolt hurtling towards my husband.

I screamed in fear for Umar's life. Thankfully, the Khan's intention was to bind him. Gold chains appeared around Umar's hands and feet. With a thud, he fell to the ground. I ran to him and cradled his head in my arms.

The Khan raised his arm at me, ready to strike ... but something extraordinary happened. My sons roared and stepped forward.

'Do not touch our mother,' said Ali, my firstborn.

Then Bilal stepped forward, and Chirag alongside him. 'Yes, you have to cross us first.'

'Yes, go through us first,' Danish chimed in.

'Your wish is my command,' said the Khan with a sneer.

Within moments, all four were on the ground, their hands and feet bound in glittering gold four-way handcuffs and foot binds.

'Royal blood is rare,' the Khan said matter-of-factly. 'It cannot be spilled needlessly. I have much use for your blood. I am going to make an example

The brothers A, B, C and D, a.k.a. Ali, Bilal, Chirag and Danish, had finally awakened from their entitled stupor. A round of applause, please, for this rare and unexpected act of bravery and valour from the erstwhile losers.

of you all!' Then he turned to me. 'I think you may be more sensible than my brother. Take care of him and tell him to listen to me or I will not hesitate to bury him alive.'

With that, he set up a cage in the middle of the Square where Umar had first stood up to the Khan. He remembered it all, this evil man. He did not imprison me in the cage with my family, but shackled my feet in gold fetters, so I could fetch food and water for Umar and my boys. There was no question, of course, of my running away and leaving my family behind. He said that I, a mere woman, was no threat to him, and he laughed at my tears. Then he put Bassam in charge and disappeared.

For two weeks, I was separated from my family. Unable to do anything to free them, I walked back to the palace over and over again to beg the royal kitchen and the harem for leftovers and scraps to feed them. But the guards did not let me enter. At times, kind passers-by would help me by bringing some food or a bottle of water. It felt like the whole world had come crashing down. I saw no hope. Prayers were my only solace.

And then, my Zeba returned.

When I see Zeba again, the sun is so strong, it is difficult to keep my eyes open.

She walks into the Square, her hijab flying majestically behind her, and frees Umar and my boys from the cage. Her father and brothers are gaping at her transformation while the people of Khudir cheer her on.

She stands in the middle of the Square and declares that not just her family but all of Khudir is now free. She urges everyone, including the soldiers guarding the Square, to join her in celebrating a 'Free Khudir!'. Most of them join her happily and start raising slogans in her support.

The overconfident Bassam, put in charge of handling the situation by his father, has been lazing in the palace, cuddling up to his newly (and rather hastily) wed wife. When he is informed about the uprising, he comes rushing to stop Zeba. But my blessed daughter simply extends her hand and freezes him and the handful of soldiers accompanying him in the middle of the Square.

Zeba stands tall in the middle of the Square, the greatest symbol of the Resistance, her entire family around her, safe and sound. The people of Khudir surround her and chant her name.

'ZEBA! ZEBA! ZEBA!'

Everyone wants a Free Khudir, and now they demand it openly.

The sound of a trumpet blowing can be heard from the palace. It comes from the Harem Quarters. It seems the West Wing of the palace has opened its gates for the first time. Women in the harem are rejoicing. Everyone is ecstatic.

Yet, there is fear too. Everyone knows that the celebrations are momentary. It is true that the Great Khan has yet to make his appearance, but his absence is now more oppressive than his physical presence. We know in our hearts that the Final War between the Great Khan and Zeba, the final face-off, is still to come. When he shows up, we must be ready.

Back in the palace, I dread the thought of this battle. My Zeba going up against the vicious Khan. Only one of them will walk away victorious. I watch my daughter make plans. So clear and specific, so completely in charge.

But while the city prepares for the big battle, Zeba wants all of us—her family, and the women and children in the harem—to be taken to safety. She does not want us getting hurt. She does not want a single drop of innocent blood to be shed, if possible. To smuggle the women and children out of the country as quickly as possible, trained pilots are summoned and asked to prepare. They plan to use the Khan's and Umar's private planes. The Gulfstream G280, Bombardier BD-700 and the Dreamliner are fuelled, stocked and readied.

Kherun is always by her side, keeping a watchful eye on her. I know that the trusted Kherun is prepared to die for my child. I am seeing her after so many years. I remember Kherun from when I first arrived in Khudir as a young bride. I remember her helping me when my youngest, Danish, was born and I developed complications during labour. Despite there being an army of midwives and doctors, Kherun had remained steadfast by my side, a constant, reassuring presence. She was always kind to all women despite the fact that the Khan often ordered her to do his nasty deeds. I trust her implicitly. It gives me comfort knowing my Zeba has people next to her who love her and will guard her with their lives.

A visitor is announced. It is the enigmatic Sultana.

Does this woman glide? I mean, we must be of the same age, but she moves like an ageless gazelle. The Sultana has come to Zeba with a request. A meeting has been requested by the Khan's younger son, Sayed.

This could be a trap, I whisper to Zeba. But Zeba does not think so.

While Bassam, the current heir, is a younger version of the Khan, with the same temperament, ambition and streak of cruelty, Sayed is different. Zeba talks about the night she overheard a drunk Sayed lamenting the situation in the country. He is an idealist who loves his country. Zeba likes him but she also feels unsure about his ability to stand up to his father. Men too have it hard, I suppose, in their own way. They have to pretend to be tough all the time in this dog-eat-dog world. Fight like a Spartan, or shut up and suffer. Brutal and heartless either way. But Sayed seems honest and earnest, gentle and kind. He wants to do the right thing. We seldom value softness in human beings but it is what the world needs more of rather than sheer aggression. Sayed has been running humanitarian programmes for people in the kingdom, trying to save the thousands that his father has oppressed. When people were starving and rioting in parts of the country, the Great Khan turned a blind eye, but Sayed did everything he could to help those in need.

The guard announces the young prince's entry, and Sayed walks in and bows respectfully. Zeba returns the gesture.

'Sister, you have freed our people from Father,' he says. 'You have brought a lot of hope to the common people on the street. I salute you.'

An uncomfortable silence follows. Zeba has never been at ease with compliments.

Sayed clears his throat and continues, 'They say you have been touched by the holy water ... that you are our saviour.'

'Apparently,' mutters Zeba.

'I must be honest with you, Sister. I have but one fear.'

Zeba raises her eyebrows.

Allah! Is he is going to fight her for the throne?

Sayed says, 'Often, the world over, what starts as a well-meaning revolution turns into tyranny. People struggle to overthrow tyrants and after they succeed suddenly find that they are ruled by yet another despot. Popular uprisings do not stop to ask common people what they really need. I need to know ... Are you going to be different, Sister?'

Zeba replies, 'I don't really want to get involved. My aim is to get my family and others out of here. I want to go home. I want to go back to America. Here, my family is not safe. They are not safe, Sayed.'

Sayed seems to have drifted off into his own thoughts. He speaks almost wistfully. 'My Khudir has seen a lot of devastation. This country is neatly divided into the uber rich and extremely poor. We have no middle class. Father made sure of that. The rich stuff themselves and the poor die of starvation. Do you know how soul-wrenching it is to witness this every day? These people are never sure where their next morsel will come from. While we live like this ... our food, our luxuries ... This uncertainty about whether it is all tainted with the blood of an innocent villager tears me apart. I seek penance every day for my life. I often travel away from the palace to pray, meditate and write ... just to be able to breathe more peacefully.'

Bless him, Allah, for his heart.

'Father has been involved in a kind of guerrilla *war against everybody*. He hates everyone. He runs our small kingdom while pretending to be an ally of America. He even let the Americans have a military base in Khudir. But he has secretly run and funded a huge network of *jihadi* outfits who are responsible for some of the biggest attacks all over the world. Abba's well-connected, well-funded network is also responsible for kidnapping journalists, photographers, tourists ... basically anyone with a foreign passport. He encourages his army of thugs to torture the hostages and release horrific videos. I am sure you must have seen some of them.'

'Yes,' replied Zeba, 'I have.'

'I come to you with an offering. Take this.'

He extends his hands and gives Zeba a beautiful shawl. Its intricate geometric patterns are so exquisite that no man could have made it. Zeba eyes widen as she recognizes it immediately.

'This is the Chaddor of Khudir,' says Sayed. 'A family heirloom, a magic shield. It is worn only by the King of Khudir. Ideally, after Father, I should inherit it. But ...' his voice trails off, 'Father will not rest till he has finished you off. He will not rest till all of Khudir is devastated. He will not rest till all the countries of the world burn in his wrath. You are the only one who can defeat him. But even you will need protection. You will need support. My sister, you will need this, the Chaddor, to defeat Father.'

I can see the hesitation in Zeba's eyes. I know what she is thinking. She does not have any intention of becoming the ruler of Khudir. She only wants to fight the Khan and get everyone to safety. Accepting the Chaddor will change this. The Chaddor is not just a magical artefact; it is a state symbol. If she accepts it and wears it, then she will have announced her claim as the leader of the people. She will not just be fighting her father in a battle for life and death, she will also be staking her claim to the throne.

While she is preoccupied with her thoughts, Sayed continues. 'But I must warn you. The Chaddor does not fully yield to everyone. The Khan wore it, but he was never able to access its full magic. Even so, it made him the most powerful man in Khudir. I'm hoping you, Sister, will make a better and more deserving master as you fight Father's might.'

Sayed extends his arms and holds the Chaddor like an offering before her. Everyone watches Zeba with bated breath. But before my child can react or do anything to accept the offering, matters are taken out of her hands. *The Chaddor flies to Zeba* and drapes itself around her shoulders. Everyone in the room gasps. I, too, am taken by surprise, to say the least.

If there was ever any doubt that Zeba was meant to save us all, it evaporates in an instant. As soon as the Chaddor touches her it settles over her shoulders and changes colour. From a pale pink, it blossoms into a flaming, shimmering gold. No one has seen the Chaddor do this before, certainly not when the Khan wore it.

Everyone around Zeba is suddenly on one knee, as is the land's custom. *Salute the Sovereign,* they say in unison. Even Sayed is taken aback, but he joins everyone in bowing down to Zeba.

Then he stands up to say, 'I had come to ask you to use the Chaddor to defeat the Khan. I believed you would defeat Father and then take your family to safety, return to America, your home, and I would be the ruler that Khudir needs. I came to you to ask you to be an ally when I rule this kingdom once the dust settles.'

Is he going to fight her, I think in panic. But before my worry sets in, he smiles.

'I was wrong. I am not the rightful heir to rule this kingdom. You are. You are the true ruler of Khudir. The Chaddor has chosen you.'

'Um, I don't think so ...' Zeba mumbles. 'Like I said, living here forever was never a part of my plan. I want to go back home after all this is over. You be King, Sayed. It will suit you. Anyway, isn't there a law that says women can't be rulers here ...?'

Sultana interjects. 'That is not true. This kingdom was ruled first by a woman many centuries ago. The first Akhoon was a woman—Amina. She was the predecessor of all the great kings born into the dynasty. But it was ensured that a tainted version of her history is remembered. Her legacy was belittled and many people, not just the Khan, tried to remove it from our records and history books.'

She walks up to Zeba. 'You see, it is always easy to tarnish the female sovereign with tales of incompetence, jealousy, vanity ... Everyone loves that sort of character assassination. Some said Amina had an affair with one of her slaves. She was portrayed as a stupid woman who chanced upon power, was seduced by a slave and eventually overthrown by her brother. It is untrue, but it made for a great story.'

'I remember this story, too,' I say. 'I heard it from my grandmother long ago. It was her favourite night-time tale.'

Sayed clears his throat and says, 'It will be my honour to help you ... um ... assist you in ruling Khudir, Queen Zeba.'

I see the colour drain from my daughter's face.

But to me it is an incredible moment. An honour beyond all. A moment of victory. The Kingdom of Khudir is about to have a female ruler, and it is my daughter.

Queen Zeba!

The importance of this historic moment is not lost on anyone. The women rejoice. There is hope. *Umeed.*

Insha Allah.

22

Musings of a Gentle Soul

She is like a snowflake. Perfect, unique, distinct. Pure. My Zeba.

Yes, I am a practising Muslim. Yes, I love America. And yes, life after 9/11 has been hard, very hard. I have felt persecuted for the name I have, for how I look. But New York is my home, my life. I'm not going to leave just because some people are stupid and misinformed.

The 9/11 attack on innocents broke my heart. It has tainted the world, divided it. Everyone around me was troubled by the same questions: *Is Islam compatible with the liberal values of the West. Is Islam compatible with my chosen home? Do I have to choose between the two?*

I knew my answer.

My home, my life is in New York. No matter what. I am an American citizen now. And proudly so. Yes, there are things about my country which make me sad. But no land is perfect. I can no longer live in my birth country Khudir. Cannot bear it now.

My brother twisted the tenets of Islam to justify his greed, his bloodlust. So, he could justify his crimes, the wars he started. The abuse and bastardization of Islam has to stop. My Islam is not what the Khan and his cronies have made it out to be.

My god is not cruel and full of hate. My god is kind and merciful.

God Is Great! *Allah Hu Akbar!*

But religion can be weak, at the mercy of power-hungry people. Prone to misappropriation and blatant lies. I mean, wasn't there a theory that linked reading Ayn Rand books to the JFK assassination? You cannot possibly blame *Atlas Shrugged* for a madman pumping a bullet through Kennedy's heart. Perhaps not quoting it here might be a better idea. Both Rand and Kipling confuse me. Should I not like them or even quote them because of their off-colour and bigoted views on many things? Or is it okay and socially acceptable to quote them on certain matters? I mean, a clock that stops working still gives the correct time twice a day, right?

When in doubt, I always ask this: Is the Quran a dangerous text? Or are there people with ignoble, ulterior motives who have spread mis-readings of it? People with impure hearts will find filth even in paradise.

EATS SHOOTS AND LEAVES.

EATS, SHOOTS, AND LEAVES.

Get it?

Because, yes, there are sociopaths like my brother, my own flesh, who use religion, use the Quran for their own gain.

Once upon a time, I hoped and prayed for redemption for him. But I have come to accept that he has changed forever on his path towards greed and ambition. No amount of reason or emotion will make sense anymore. He is beyond all that. The only way to combat him? My little snowflake. My little Zeba.

I have always thought of her as a snowflake. Perfect, unique, pure.

I once saw a snowflake under the microscope and was amazed by its complexity, its brilliance, its distinctiveness. The unique thing about snowflakes is that they grow as they fall. They are so fragile, yet they thrive as they descend through the air to the ground. Just like my Zeba. Her pain helps her grow and metamorphose. She is unique and complex, yet her heart is pure and untainted. That is why whenever I think of a snowflake it reminds me of my daughter.

But, I am sad today.

Perhaps, when this day is done, I shall never see my child again. But I know one thing in my heart. It is my Zeba's destiny to grow constantly as she goes through life's hardest lessons.

May Allah give her the strength.

23

Hope Where There Was None

How did these women, always in purdah, always separated, exercise so much influence in this post-9/11 world of Khudir and the US of A that brought about the end of the Biggest Despot of the Modern World??

This is what I want the world to ask when all this is done and dusted. That should be the title of the first chapter of OUR BOOK. I want our story, the story of our glittering yet shadowy world, of our harem ... to be read and remembered. But this time it will be different. This time, we will write the narrative ourselves.

The world finds us *harem women* so enigmatic, alluring, mysterious. Perhaps, many think of us as slaves—voiceless and submissive. Yet, they do not know who we are and the role we have played over the years. It's simpler for them to label us as weak, imprisoned, cunning, ambitious, nagging, sexy. Or, sister, wife, mother, keep, whore.

From time immemorial, the only people to have written about us are men. Men recorded our stories, our histories. Took over our narrative. Reimagined our lives, our inner worlds ... all from their own prism. I walk towards the West Wing to retrieve my almost finished manuscript: ***Forgotten Queens and Female Leaders of Khudir***. It is about the women who fought the system. The women who triumphed despite the times they were born in. The women who were denied the right to rule, to fight in battle, to hold a title or even read a book. But who did not take no for an answer. They were all fighters, real leaders who refused to bow down. Today, little is known about these women, and what little is available is such an ugly, sanitized version of their lives that it makes me sick.

The uniqueness of these queens, their complexity, everything has been taken apart, beaten out of these narratives. They have been boiled down into something that is easy for men to comprehend. Pigeonholed and made palatable; some easily available label attached. Black and white. Bitch and whore.

But that is not what I want to do. I do not want to simply record their lives and their stories. I want to celebrate their uniqueness, their distinctive jagged edges. Who were they really on the inside? The whole deal. Not some airbrushed version of it. I want to honour the memory of these warriors. I want their sacrifices to be known so that their lives were not lived in vain. They contributed. They made a difference. They were loved. They were respected.

It has been my life's work, writing about these women whose tales I have heard in hushed voices as a little girl but whose histories I spent my whole adult life trying to study. I have immersed myself in writing and researching this book. This is my legacy.

I want to unveil the book at the crowning ceremony of our new Queen.

Queen Zeba.

A diamond in the rough. A *heera* with jagged edges.

But I must hurry. Thoughts are such mischievous things. They constantly transport you to another place and make you lose all sense of the work at hand.

So much is still to be done. We have had an exciting couple of weeks. Some incredible things have unfolded, all of which shall find mention in my book—in the final chapter perhaps. They have to. After all, history has been made.

For now, we have a coronation to plan. There is much to do. How can we make it grand without seeming extravagant; symbolic without being too indulgent; reflect tradition while looking forward to progressive changes?

Ah! Indeed, there is *much to do.*

Along with Zeba's coronation we must also perform a ceremony for Sayed. I wonder what title we should give him to rightly reflect his importance in Khudir. Commander of the Realm? President? Prime Minister? It must be significant, yet second to Zeba. Zeba cannot not be reduced to a figurehead, but we must also do right by Sayed. Chronicle the sacrifices he has made. Acknowledge that it takes a special person to allow for such radical change to take place.

Oh Sayed! You blessed boy, you lovely soul. I saw you fight every day against the Khan and his ideology. I watched you silently bear all the humiliations yet never give up. I am so proud of you. And you should be proud of yourself.

Sayed has blossomed into such a kind young man, such a compassionate soul. I recall his youthful years—painting miniatures and writing Sufi poetry were his burning passions. I must admit, I was afraid he would grow up to be lazy and conceited like his siblings. Or just evil, like Bassam. But he has selflessly done what no prince-in-waiting would have the *jigar* to do. He has given Zeba the Chaddor, the key to Khudir. He has told all his men and soldiers to take Zeba's side and yield to her calling. He has made so much of this happen.

Thank you, son. Today, in Khudir, men stand side by side with women to fight for freedom. Freedom and respect for all. It is something this land I was born in has never seen before.

As practising Muslims, we know that God Almighty has sent many Prophets over the ages to show humankind the Righteous Path. Mohammad (Peace Be Upon Him) was the last Prophet sent to guide people and gift them God's final word in the Quran. But does that mean that no one will come to guide us again? To save us? Does that mean that we do not need to be saved anymore? Or that perhaps, *nau-zu-billah*, even God has abandoned us?

Over the years, I have often prayed to God Almighty to save us from the Khan, from the darkness of his heart, from his evil designs. Dreading the day, he may invoke his dark magic and call forth the Devil, the messenger of Shaitan himself—Yazoo. I have prayed fervently. Fasted. Undertaken many a Haj. I have fought the best I can. Risked my life often. Helped poor Kherun and her scruffy Army of the Pure. Ensured many disadvantaged souls made it across the borders to safety. Saved villages from the wrath of the Khan. I, and everyone on this journey with me, we did all of this fearlessly, knowing that we were on the right path. We were ... we are ready to embrace death with a smile on our lips.

Fear does not suit Sultana indeed.

But there were many moments of self-doubt still. How were we ever going to be saved? Who could protect us? Come to our rescue?

At times like those, I drew strength from the women and men of Khudir who had stood with us. We are in this together. God may not send us another Prophet, but he will always watch over us and protect us. This is the faith that has kept us going. Whether Zeba can save us or not, we are happy to die fighting by her side. That is the power of believing in something bigger than yourself. That is the power of doing the Right Thing.

As I walk past BiBi, who is carefully selecting her post-lunch paan, I cannot help but smile. She gave me such an outrageous interview for my book a few years ago before her Alzheimer's set in. This woman is a riot. Her anecdotes about the long line of Akhoon kings are deliciously scandalous. It is a pity that she is no longer able to comprehend what is happening around her. It would have made her happy to know that her prediction has come true in her lifetime: Khudir will finally be ruled by a Queen.

I ask the servants to summon all the ladies of the house. A call has gone out to the entire West Wing, including the secret chambers. Everyone is getting ready. The coronation is only a few hours away, and the air is full of excitement.

A few of my fellow sisters, who fancy themselves poetesses, are flapping about trying to write quick sonnets in praise of the new Queen. Others are busy deciding their attires. What does one wear to the coronation of the Queen of Khudir?

I smile as I extract from my locker my prized possession, my handwritten manuscript, and wrap it in piece of a gorgeous satin cloth.

Suddenly, without warning, the sky grows dark. I have never seen the likes of it—purple and then black. As if someone has turned off the lights in the world, as though without warning the sun has gone into a total eclipse. Birds turn around and fly homewards, thinking that perchance the day is over. A sinister wind blows in our direction. Stars appear in the sky but they do not twinkle. A heaviness descends, like a dense invisible fog that is incredibly suffocating.

I hear a scream. My heart sinks.

My personal guard comes running, breathless and panting. 'Yazoo is at the palace gates!' he wheezes out.

'NO!' I yell so loudly that the guard staggers back in shock.

We have waited for this day for a while now. *Allah reham*. The Lord have mercy.

24

The Big Battle

Location

The gates of Khudir's Royal Palace, the spectral silhouette of the edifice looming ominously against the darkening sky, an island of silhouetted spires and domes in a sea of uncertainty.

Main Cast

Yazoo. Freshly resurrected messenger of Shaitan, the greatest evil force EVER. (I know, we've established that already.) A figure of unspeakable power, his resplendent aura of darkness pulsating like an abyss, sucking in any shred of hope or valour. Under no man's control any longer, but still bound by the Laws of Magic to destroy Zeba. A serious threat to Zeba's life.

The Khan. A mumbling, whistling pumpkin-brain. Comatose, vegetative. Little more than a pitiful husk, an eerie reminder of the horrifying consequences of human greed. A powerful symbol of Yazoo's damaging capabilities, a living testament to his terrifying power.

Zeba. Yet to be coronated Queen-in-Waiting, possessor of superpowers bestowed upon her by the holy spring Zsa Zsa, master of the Chaddor, and commander of Khudir's army led by Sayed. Still a novice at this save-the-world/superhero thing and suffering miserably from imposter syndrome, her own monster within.

The Universally Preferred Outcome

Zeba, the Superhero, wins. The Supervillain is defeated once and for all. The Great Khan is a vegetable in a care home, a chilling example of what happens to nasty, greedy people. Everyone else lives happily ever after.

But we all know that for any good story there must be a ...

TWIST IN THE TALE!

A Sudden Turn of Events to raise the stakes and make the climax juicier.

So ... Yazoo gets inside Zeba's head and uses her greatest vulnerability.

When that decisive moment comes and Zeba and Yazoo come face to face, everything blurs away in the background. Yazoo's form begins to distort. His menacing shape dissolves into another softer, more familiar outline. Before Zeba's disbelieving eyes, Yazoo morphs into the image of her departed mother, Miriam.

Zeba is torn and her heart beats like a war drum, her blood runs cold and her hands tremble. This emotional war is more crippling, more lethal than any physical assault.

Yazoo has cornered Zeba. She is no longer fighting with him on the battlefield of the palace gates; the fight is now taking place in the corridors of her heart and the chambers of her mind.

What will she do? Conflict rages within ...

Zeba is terrified. How will she attack her dead mother?

25

The Final Chapter

Due to the author's personal issues with violence, this chapter has been left to the reader's imagination and/or discretion. Please feel free to imagine as much violence, blood and gore as is possible. No censorship rules apply.

Another honest admission: Many bestselling authors (not just J.K. Rowling) and blockbuster action-film directors (apart from Zack Snyder and Rohit Shetty) have set the bar so high for what passes for a good climax that the author may have chickened out from even attempting to write it. The fear of writing a dowdy anti-climax sent the author into uncontrollable spasms and anxiety, which almost led to a complete collapse.

Given above are a few reasons for the omission of this chapter. Please choose your favourite answer. Whatever you want to believe, please believe at your own peril.

The author regrets shattering any expectations vis-à-vis a fulfilling Final Battle that the reader had formed while reading the earlier chapters of this book.

Of course, in the end ... yada yada yada ... Zeba defeats Yazoo.

And everyone lives happily ever after.

26

Six months later

The Aftermath

You know how some say that coitus that follows a massive world-saving combat feels so *freaking* good? Well, this is a first for me, and it is the best climax I've ever had. I mean orgasm. (Also, I've realized that a good orgasm always depends way more on you than it does on the other person.) Lesson learnt. So, it's not about cute face or smile; it's about you, honey.

Inhale. Smoke. Sex. Smoke. Bliss. Exhale.

I'm going to quit smoking. I have to. It's not good for me. The nicotine and tar. And I'm going to shed five pounds. Those last five that just refuse to melt away. Yes, even superheroes can have body image issues, okay? Note to self: Need to hire Chris Hemsworth's trainer.

I think I need to take a walk. Clear my head. Get some steps in. Apparently ten thousand steps is the new magic number. Amazing! Do anything ten thousand times, and you become good at it. Should I take up guitar lessons? Sorry ... That was a random thought.

It's not going to be easy, I know, to unsee, unthink, what I've been through. Some battle scars are too deep. Some perhaps never heal.

I also know that I'm a prime candidate for PTSD. The flashes have started. I feel waves of nausea come and go. And guilt.

So much fucking guilt.

No one is taking me seriously here. Dude, **PTSD** is a **serious** mental condition that some people develop after a shocking or **dangerous** event. And what happened to me was fucking terrifying. Freaking traumatic. But I don't think anyone in Khudir has heard of PTSD. Or wants to acknowledge it. They think it's some privileged, First World disease. They just want me to get over it. And move on. Stay focused on the larger picture. For the greater good.

Blah blah blah.

Argh. Give me a break! I want to slap someone. This is not just me being disgruntled. You can't just get me a cupcake and a furry puppy, and hope this will go away. I won't smile and say thank you and get better spontaneously.

I'm sad. Very fucking sad. Is there a word sadder than sad? Then I'm that. And I'm angry. I'm sad–angry multiplied by ten thousand. And one question keeps nagging at me: If this superhero thing is a long-term plan then **will I always feel so bad after saving the world?**

So many people dead. Gone. Because of me. *Shitty me.* I don't even want to be their Queen. Never did. But they didn't know that. They just pulled an act-first-think-later and fucking ran into battle and died. For what? For me.

Fuck! Why? Why didn't I get a choice in the matter?

Dude, seriously. Yazoo burnt half the city. Most of the palace. The library, the garden. Schools. Buildings. Shit that took years and money to build ... just gone. He destroyed the museum. So many priceless objects, erased. Forever.

List of the affected?

1. Kherun, dead. Trying to protect me. Trying to save me. Took a bullet for me. More like a lightning bolt.
2. Sultana, dead. She handed me a book that was her life's work. She asked me to be a good queen, and to get the book published. Sayed and I just finalized the cover last week. We want to release it next month—six months after she was slain. But if I tell you about the book deal you will laugh. No money in publishing. A woman's life's work can't even buy you an Hermes Birkin. Something is really wrong with the world.
3. My brother Chirag is left without a toe. Actually, that may not be such a big deal after all. He has this phantom toe thing going on. But I want to honour his loss, his offering to the cause.
4. Amma had a close shave. She was in a coma for two weeks. How would I have ever hoped to forgive myself if she had died? The woman who took care of me and raised me ... gave me love. My palms are sweaty just thinking about it.
5. The prisoners kept in the dungeon ... Some of them drowned in their cells. Drowned. Only one superhero around here shooting water jets from her hands and creating mini tsunamis. Moi. This thing ... this superpower. I cannot control it. Not totally, anyway. All the water jets that missed Yazoo didn't have a place to go. So much water seeped into the dungeon and killed those poor souls. Fourteen people were found floating in their cell.

> And sure ... they were all genuinely bad dudes who deserved to die. But still, I killed them. I had no right to. They did me no wrong. They had no fight with anyone. I had no right to be the cause of their death.

It could have been Abba. What if it had been his cell?

I had to lay Kherun and Sultana to rest. This time in marked graves, next to my Ammi's unmarked one.

We gave them a good send off. At least they had both led full lives. The plan is to have a memorial site built for them so that their names and contribution will never be forgotten. I think the Square would be apt, but I must discuss it with the Royal Engineer. Or perhaps I should let Sayed handle it. He is good at that stuff. And I should get Miriam Ammi a tombstone at least. Khudir can do that much. For the Queen's birth mother.

Honestly, all I want to do is forget all of this and just go home.

No, that is not possible.

They want me to stay. Even though I don't know what I'm doing or what I should do next. Shining one day in the battlefield, being a hero for one lucky day is one thing. But being a leader to a country of people? That's a whole different ballgame.

I'm not cut out for this shit.

What happens when people come to me to sort their shit out or give them advice? I can't do that. I'm not good at advice. Heck, I always need some myself.

I need to go someplace and be really sad. Just super sad. Maybe I'll go to India. They say it's a spiritual land of peace or something. Go ride some elephants, hang with yogis, play with deer and whatever exotic beasts they have there, eat some vegan food, detox in general.

Fuck fuck fuck!

I'm going to have to deal with all this bloody anxiety and despair and sadness. I haven't been able to sleep for more than four hours at a stretch. I'd love to just stay in bed and smoke my doobie and eat–sleep–repeat. But they keep involving me in everything.

I hate adulting. And I hate superhero-ing. Can I get a few weeks or months off? Get away from Khudir? Avoid people? Mom and Sayed, for starters. Their positivity and optimism about a better future for 'our people' is getting on my nerves. I do not want to rebuild Khudir. I want to howl and weep.

We fucked up. I fucked up. People died. Kherun died. I ... I ... I was made to ... I attacked *my mother*!

That fucking Yazoo ... They said he takes the form of your biggest fear or weakness in human form. But I wasn't prepared for *that*. The worst I imagined was a giant spider or an Amazonian lizard. (I do hate lizards *and* spiders.) But the asshole took the form of my mother. My dead Miriam Ammi!

I have never felt such fear and agony all at once. It was the worst form of pain imaginable. Attacking and trying to kill your mother has got to fuck you up emotionally, right? Even if you know that it can't possibly be her.

But in that moment, Yazoo created a scenario such that I didn't know what was real and what was not. It was like a weird mushroom trip, where the painting on the wall moves only when you look at it straight up and head-on. I think I'm going to take a long time to get back to being okay. It's not going to be easy. To get all this out of my head. That asshole Yazoo won even in his defeat.

Oh! And let's not forget, seeing my dad, my biological father acting like a loon ... that was messed up too. Even though he was a bat-shit-crazy dictator, I kept holding out on the hope that maybe ... just maybe ... we could save him.

Don't get me wrong. I hated him. I still hate him. The Khan and everything he stood for was *despicable*. He was everything wrong and bad in the world all rolled into a mass of bone and skin and fat. But when I saw the blabbering mess of a man he had become, I did feel a surge of pity.

The fight was hard emotional shit, and at one point the ball was in my court. At one point, I could have killed the Khan. Very easily. Yet I hesitated. In that final moment, I'm ashamed to admit, I faltered. What was it? The knowledge that perhaps he was not always such a total monster. After all, from what Kherun told me, he was a little boy who was hurt so bad that he wanted to hurt the world back. A little boy who had lost everything. His home, his father, his life, his family ... everything was taken away from him.

In my heart, I kept asking, 'Could that little boy still be alive inside this mad tyrant? Can he still be saved?'

The Khan did bad shit. Period. But bad shit had happened to him too. Period. And then, the old bad shit made him do worse shit in the present. A fucked-up cycle.

And in that moment of hesitation, we could have lost. If I had waited a second longer, I would have been dead on the ground. That Yazoo would have taken my head. The bastard was pretty good at exploding heads.

A vivid reel of exploding heads is playing again in my mind. Ugh! Sorry, Sultana. Not an elegant departure for you.

But, if bad stuff happens to you, does that give you a license to be an asshole?

No, sir. Nope.

Pause. Breathe. In. Out. Inhale. 1 2 3 4 5 6 7 8. Hold. 1 2 3 4. Exhale. 1 2 3 4 5 6 7 8 9 10.

Moral of the story? Keep your shit together when in battle (and in general).

No hesitation. No mercy. That is my biggest learning. Often, in life, there are moments of crisis, of not knowing which direction you should take. All that matters in that situation is to keep pressing on and be true to yourself. Do the Right Thing no matter how hard it gets. *No hesitation. No mercy.* I think I did the right thing. Overall, I mean. Took the right decisions despite being petrified on the inside.

I grew up in New York, rich, free and 'not oppressed', so I know what freedom and privilege mean. I admit I was/am a selfish kid who grew up not knowing anything beyond my primary concerns. I had no idea how more than half the world lives and what problems they deal with. But I do now. Not everyone is free. (And definitely not rich.)

But perhaps, because I am a woman, I now have a different kind of power—the power to inspire, that is. Perhaps others will realize that if I can do what I have done, so can they. If Zeba—as messed up, fucked up and lost as she is—can be a superhero, so can anyone else. Right?

Since the day of the war, I've had this weird dream over and over.

Ammi—I mean Miriam—comes to me and, sounding like a hoarse man on acid, says, 'It's not over yet.' She says Yazoo is not *gone* gone.

He is going to send us a plague. A plague that will destroy us and that I will have to stop it from spreading.

I'm not even sure if I should take this dream-vision seriously. Should I just ignore it as the rumblings of an exhausted mind? Could it be an omen of some sort? Or just my overactive imagination?

I must go see BiBi today. After the battle, she gave me a weird gift. That woman is a bit nuts, though she has some serious chess moves.

First, while I was weeping in front of her as she whipped my ass with her chess moves, she said her first word to me: FLY ... Or something that sounded like GO FLY. What did she mean, I wonder. She wouldn't say another word when I asked her.

Then she reached under her chair and brought out her gift. A hijab. A hijab made not of the traditional black cloth but royal blue.

It's cute but where am I supposed to wear it? On my next adventure, I suppose. Shall I try flying as well? Jump off a building and hope to glide in the air? I think I might be too chicken for that kind of peril.

I'm so tired, man. I hope this is it. The first and last time I have to save the world. This shit is exhausting. I don't think I can fight any more bad guys, or wizards, or armies, or plagues or pandemics. Or whatever is coming next.

I just *cannot.*

I have no will left to ... **fight. And win.**

I need to speak to Dr Singh ... I'm sure superheroes need a therapist too, right?

Acknowledgements

There are a lot of people I need to thank.

But let's go chronologically ...

First, Deepa Mehta, who thought I could write and am smart. Both of which I still highly doubt. But since you have turned to this page, maybe she has a point.

Sarita Tanwar, for being in my corner. And being the best didi anyone can ask for. (Please pronounce 'didi' like the cool south Delhi girls say it.☺) She has done more for me than she knows.

Bilal Siddiqui, for telling me to stop being lazy and write. And having endless cups of black coffee while coaxing me to meet his publisher buddies and send my manuscript to them.

Twinkle Khanna, for being her! A champion of girl power, with sharp wit and gorgeous cascading hair. Thank you for reading my initial chapters and encouraging me and introducing me to my now agent.

My agent Hemali Sodhi at A Suitable Agency, for always being there and helping me navigate the complex and tediously slow world of publishing. Did I mention underpaid?

Swati Daftuar, for being my first editor. She loved this book and saw its potential. I can never thank her enough. Oh! And for being the most talkative editor ever. And Sonal Nerurkar, for introducing us. Bless you all!

Poulomi Chatterjee, for helping me make this book better. She has vastly improved my voice and helped me crystallize my thoughts.

The whole team at HarperCollins India, for being such champions of this book. Can't believe they liked what they read. I don't want to show anyone that red-track document they sent back. For a now-published author, I clearly can't punctuate! 🙈

Pia, who designed this wonderful cover and did all the inside illustrations. Her work makes this book even more special.

My team at Collective and Pearl Media, for supporting all my dreams and wild ambitions as an artist. Like writing a book while working a full-fledged acting job. Nuts!

My narcissistic ex, for reading the whole damn thing and saying he loved it. Meant a lot at that time.

That tech support guy at Petit Ermitage in LA, for sorting my laptop out in March 2023, else I would have never made my deadline. Yes, I am technologically challenged.

All the amazing directors and writers I've had the pleasure of working and collaborating with, for making me understand the power of storytelling.

All my friends, who were forced to read some sections only so I could see their reaction to certain chapters. My beloved guinea pigs.

RS, who just makes me immensely happy and safe.

My brother, Saqib, for being my constant—constant support and constant pain in the ass.

My mom and dad. And Streak.

I love you all.

Blessed.

ABOUT THE AUTHOR

Huma S Qureshi, a kebab-seller's daughter who likes to think of herself as Kebab Royalty of south Delhi, was an outsider who became a star in the glittering world of the Hindi film industry. She has charted her own career path and, in defiance of her naysayers, has acted in Hindi and regional (now pan-India) films, shows on streaming platforms and international films. In 2022, Huma embarked on a new chapter by starting her own production house, Elemen3. She continues her (self-proclaimed) trailblazing journey with this book, her debut work as an author. Now there is no filter between her thoughts and the rest of the world ... God bless us all!

HarperCollins *Publishers* India

At HarperCollins India, we believe in telling the best stories and finding the widest readership for our books in every format possible. We started publishing in 1992; a great deal has changed since then, but what has remained constant is the passion with which our authors write their books, the love with which readers receive them, and the sheer joy and excitement that we as publishers feel in being a part of the publishing process.

Over the years, we've had the pleasure of publishing some of the finest writing from the subcontinent and around the world, including several award-winning titles and some of the biggest bestsellers in India's publishing history. But nothing has meant more to us than the fact that millions of people have read the books we published, and that somewhere, a book of ours might have made a difference.

As we look to the future, we go back to that one word—a word which has been a driving force for us all these years.

Read.